Other Books by Brian Doyle

BOY O'BOY

THE LOW LIFE

MARY ANN ALICE

UNCLE RONALD

SPUD IN WINTER

SPUD SWEETGRASS

COVERED BRIDGE

EASY AVENUE

UP TO LOW

YOU CAN PICK ME UP AT PEGGY'S COVE

HEY, DAD!

Angel Square

ANGEL SQUARE

Brian Doyle

A GROUNDWOOD BOOK
DOUGLAS & McINTYRE
TORONTO VANCOUVER BERKELEY

New paperback edition 2003
Second printing 2004

Groundwood Books / Douglas & McIntyre Ltd.
720 Bathurst Street, Suite 500, Toronto, Ontario M5S 2R4

Distributed in the USA by Publishers Group West
1700 Fourth Street, Berkeley, CA 94710

We acknowledge for their financial support of our publishing program the Canada Council for the Arts, the Government of Canada through the Book Publishing Industry Development Program (BPIDP), the Ontario Arts Council and the Government of Ontario through the Ontario Media Development Corporation's Ontario Book Initiative.

National Library of Canada Cataloguing in Publication
Doyle, Brian
Angel Square
ISBN 0-88899-609-8
I. Title.
PS8557.O87A78 2003 jC813'.54 C2003-905823-9

Cover photograph by Tim Fuller
Design by Michael Solomon

Printed and bound in Canada

To all my family, then and now.

Caution to those with Lowertown memory:
Many proper names have been altered to fit the truth
to my fiction

TABLE OF CONTENTS

Part I

1 Let Me Tell You

LET ME TELL YOU about last Christmas. The first Christmas after the war. And let me tell you about Sammy's father.

And Margot Lane.

When I heard what happened to Sammy's father I first thought Aunt Dottie said "assassinated" but it wasn't "assassinated," it was *assaulted.* Sammy's father was assaulted. Beat up. In the streetcar barns where he worked at night. Night watchman.

Dad said he saw it in the paper. A man in a hood went into the streetcar barns and beat up Sammy Rosenberg's father the night watchman for nothing. Mr. Rosenberg told the police what he saw. Then he went into a sleep.

"It wasn't for nothing," Aunt Dottie said. "It was

because he's Jewish. Some people around here don't like you if you're Jewish."

It was coming up to the first Christmas after the war and everything was supposed to be nice from now on. And now this happened. Who would want to beat up a nice man like Sammy's father? A man in a hood. A hood made of a flour bag cut-off. The printing on the flour bag said, RITCHIE'S FEED AND SEED.

Ritchie's Feed and Seed is a store in the market next to Peter Devine's where we get our groceries. And near there is R. Hector Aubrey's where we get our meat. That's where Aunt Dottie stared so hard at Mr. Aubrey cutting the meat one time that he almost chopped his thumb off with the cleaver.

Sammy is my best school friend. We walk to school together. He lives on Cobourg Street, the same street as I live on. In Lowertown.

In Ottawa,

Ontario,

Canada,

Planet Earth,

The Universe.

December, 1945.

That was the address I put in my workbook at school. We were practising writing letters and addressing them. Letters to ourselves.

"Dear Tommy; How are you? I am fine," etc.

I asked the teacher if it would be all right if we wrote

our letter to somebody else. He said no, the best way to practice was to write to yourself and then when you got that right you'd be allowed to write to somebody else and shut up and don't be impertinent.

Impertinent.

When he saw the address in my workbook he put a big X through it and tore the paper he pressed so hard. Then he said I was stupid.

His name was Mr. Blue Cheeks.

He was the worst teacher I ever had.

I said Sammy is my best school friend. We both have to cross Angel Square to get to York Street School where we go. It is a dangerous square to cross four times a day, so it is a good thing that we have each other for protection.

There are three schools on Angel Square.

On one side is The School of Brother Brébeuf where all the French Canadians go. But nobody calls them French Canadians. Everybody calls them Pea Soups.

On the second side of Angel Square is York Street School where Sammy and I go. Most of the people who go to York Street School are Jewish. I'm not.

I'm not anything.

But nobody calls them Jewish. Everybody calls them Jews.

On the third side of the square is St. Brigit's School of the Bleeding Thorns where all the Irish Catholics go. But nobody calls them that. Everybody calls them Dogans.

So four times a day most of the Pea Soups, Jews and Dogans try to cross Angel Square to get home or go to school.

Last year was the same.

Sammy would meet me on the corner of Papineau and Cobourg at eight-thirty and we'd walk down Papineau and then try and cross the square to get to school. At twelve o'clock Sammy would meet me at the schoolyard gate. We'd walk up York Street and then try and cross Angel Square to get home for dinner. At the one o'clock signal, the sound of the long dash on the radio, I would leave our house, meet Sammy and try the square again. After school at four o'clock Sammy would meet me and we'd try and cross the square one more time to get home. Quite a job.

All the streetcars come up Cobourg Street to go to the car barns for the night. When I am in bed at night I can feel the streetcars rumbling up Cobourg Street, one after another, going home to the barns to rest.

They shake my bed as they go by. In the summer, when we go up to Low to our cabin on the Gatineau River, I can't sleep very well because it is so quiet. There are just crickets and maybe a whip-poor-will. Not nice and soothing like the thundering of streetcars.

The barns where Sammy's father was night watchman have deep pits between the tracks with stairs going down each one so the mechanics can work underneath on the cars and fix them and grease them. Each pit is coated with a pad of grease and dust which makes it like a rug, and has a light in it that you can switch on and off.

Sammy and I would play cops and robbers down in those pits with our cap guns. There are a hundred pits in the barns. Sammy and I killed many cops and robbers there.

We don't do that any more. We're too old now.

I was half asleep when I heard about Sammy's father that morning. It was Tuesday morning and Aunt Dottie was waking me up to go to school. After she and Dad told me what happened I knew then why Sammy wasn't at school the day before. I had to do Angel Square four times by myself. That's why I was so tired Monday night.

Tired and full with dreams.

Dreams of Lowertown and movies and programs on the radio and Christmas. And Margot.

In one of my dreams I heard a long scream and I knew that something had dragged the lovely Margot Lane into the swamp. I went chasing into that evil darkness, gooey things pulling at me and mud sucking me down. I came to an old cabin and saw through the window that the evil professor in his white coat had the lovely Margot Lane tied to a chair. He was holding a red-hot poker near her lovely face. Her eyes were wide and mostly white and staring up to the side like the eyes of a scared horse. In my big black hat with the big brim and my cloak I turned invisible and went in the cabin and grabbed the professor's wrist as the poker came closer.

He had a German accent. He said this:

"Vat is it ZAT ISS holdink my arm? I cannot moof my arm!"

"Oh, Shadow," sighed the lovely Margot Lane, "you've come at last. I thought you'd never get here in time to save me!"

"Your ugly game is over, Herr Professor," I said in a very low voice. "This is your last innocent swamp victim! You can't escape The Shadow! Heh heh heh heh heh heh!"

I woke up and saw Aunt Dottie standing beside my bed.

"I heard some peculiar laughing in here," she said.

"I was dreaming I was The Shadow and was in a big swamp to save Margot Lane from the evil professor," I told her through the fog of waking up.

"I shouldn't let you listen to that awful radio program any more. It's so filthy. Roaming around in swamps! Go down the cellar and feel the tank. If there's any hot water you'd better take a bath before you go to school."

I think Aunt Dottie figured I'd get dirty even dreaming.

"Do I have to? I'm not even dirty."

"Hurry up. Of course you're dirty. Everybody's dirty after dreaming. Especially about swamps! Look, I think I see mud on your elbows."

"I wasn't *on* my elbows."

"Well, your knees then. Hurry up. The Quaker is almost ready."

The Quaker. Quick Quaker Oats. My favorite stuff. Specially with brown sugar. And we had brown sugar now. Brown sugar wasn't rationed any more. The war was over.

My favorite breakfast is to sit with the Quick Quaker Oats box in front of me while I eat the hot porridge with the milk and brown sugar. I eat and listen to Dad and Aunt Dottie talking. (My sister Pamela is already at her front window.) And while I eat and listen to Dad and Aunt Dottie talking I study the picture on the Quick Quaker Oats box. I can do those three things at once. Eat, listen and study the box.

On the box is a picture of a handsome Quaker in his Quaker outfit, standing there, smiling, looking out at me. No matter how I turn the box, his eyes are always on me.

That is one thing about the Quaker. He always looks at me no matter where the box is. If I can see the Quaker anywhere, on the table, over on the window sill, on the shelf above the stove, in the cupboard, he is looking at me.

The other thing about the Quaker is that he's holding a box of Quick Quaker Oats! And of course, on the box he's holding there's a picture of himself holding a box of Quick Quaker Oats. And on that little box there's the same picture. And if I had X-ray vision like Superman I would be able to see the next little Quaker and the next one and the next one.

"Get your nose off of that box, you'll get germs," Aunt Dottie said quietly as she pulled on her white gloves to serve Dad and me some toast.

"You never know where that box has been and who might have touched it," she said.

Dad gave me a wink. Then he said this:

"I read in the paper that these boxes are untouched by human hands. They're handled with tongs in the factory and sterilized robots take them off the trucks and put them on the shelves in the store. The only human hands that might have touched the box might be the hands of Toe-Jam Laframboise."

Toe-Jam Laframboise is the delivery man who drives the grocery truck. Toe-Jam never washes much. He drives Aunt Dottie mad. Dad said Toe-Jam never washes his feet because he can't get his socks off. The blue mold has scaled his socks right to his skin.

Aunt Dottie whisked the Quaker off the table and put him outside between the doors. Maybe the cold would freeze those germs off him. I saw him smiling at me as Aunt Dottie shut him out in the cold. Good-bye all you Quakers until tomorrow. How many Quakers were there? A million, I guess. If you had eyes like Superman.

I ate my Quaker, stood over the heat in the hall for a minute and took off for school. Outside, I waved at my sister Pamela in her window and headed up Cobourg Street.

A guy across the street I knew waved at me.

"Hi, Lamont!" he shouted.

Even though my name is Tommy, they all called me Lamont. Lamont Cranston.

It was the radio program everybody used to listen to called "The Shadow," and on it, this guy, Lamont Cranston, used to make himself invisible and fight crime that way.

The program would start with The Shadow saying, "Who knows what evil LURKS in the hearts of men! *The Shadow* knows! Heh, heh, heh, heh…!" Then there'd be a lot of very scary organ music that would run all over the place then stop and then suddenly start again so sharp it would make you jump. I could just imagine the guy playing the organ, stabbing at the keys with his fingers to make me jump and hit my head on the radio. I'd hit my head because our radio didn't go up very loud sometimes because of some tubes that were burnt out or weak or something. I'd have to lie on the floor with my head stuck in between the legs of the radio so I could hear and sometimes the cat would be there with me. Sometimes the cat would purr too loud and I'd have to shove him away because I couldn't hear what was going on with The Shadow.

Then the announcer would say this:

"Years ago in the Orient, Cranston learned a strange and mysterious secret: the hypnotic power to cloud men's minds so they cannot see him.

"Cranston's friend and companion, the lovely Margot Lane, is the only person who knows to whom the voice of the invisible Shadow belongs. Today's drama: *The Devil takes a wife!*"

Organ music; bonk on the radio with my head.

Then, at the end of the program:

"Again next week, The Shadow will demonstrate that—the weed of crime bears bitter fruit. Crime does not pay. The Shadow knows! Heh heh heh heh heh...!"

Organ music.

Bonk!

The thing I haven't told you yet is this:

There was a girl I really liked in my class named Margot Lane. Everybody knew I liked her except one person.

That person was Margot Lane herself.

I turned down Papineau and looked at Angel Square. I had to cross that square to get to school.

I watched the groups of Jews running for their lives across Angel Square. Who was chasing them this time? It looked like a vicious gang of Dogans.

In the distance, away across the other side of Angel Square, a terrified gang of Pea Soups was scattering. Moving in on them was a very serious-looking bunch of Jews.

In another place on the square two Dogans had a Pea Soup down and were beating him with their hats.

Over there, two Jews were tying a Dogan to a post.

Over here, two Pea Soups were trying to tear off a Jew's arm.

Over there, three Jews and a Dogan were torturing a Pea Soup with bats.

In the center some Pea Soups were burying alive a Dogan in a deep hole in the snow.

Across there, a Pea Soup, a Jew and a Dogan had surrounded somebody they thought might be a Protestant.

Here, a Jew was beating up two other Jews.

There, six Dogans and five Pea Soups were discussing and pointing at somebody they had trapped, probably a Jew.

Over there, a Pea Soup, a Dogan and a Jew were all tangled up on the ground.

In another place on the square a group of Dogans was selling what looked like a stray Protestant to a group of Pea Soups. A Jew was acting as interpreter.

Somewhere else, two Jews were trying to unscrew a Pea Soup's head.

I started across the square. Alone—because Sammy wasn't with me. Because of his dad.

All over the square, Dogans, Pea Soups and Jews were tearing the sleeves out of one another's coats and trying to rip each other limb from limb.

Suddenly the bells from the three schools began to ring. I was lucky. I'd only had three fights. Lost two and won one. Not bad considering I was alone.

Priests and teachers were running, herding us all to our own buildings.

There was a lot of shouting and bawling. It was like runaway cattle in a movie.

Soon the square would be empty.

Only hundreds of mitts and hats and parts of coats would be left, dark patches in the white snow.

School was in.

School wasn't getting along with me very well lately. And I wasn't getting along very well with it.

It pretty well all started back when I was in Grade Five and Miss Strong just laughed at me when I said I wanted to be a writer when I grew up.

She didn't really laugh, I guess, she just made a kind of sound with her mouth like you would if you were blowing a little feather or a hunk of fluff off your upper lip just under your nose.

Or maybe it was way back in Grade Four when we had the I.Q. test. They gave all the grade fours an I.Q. test and I was the only one who had to go back the next day and do it over again. I saw Miss Frack and Miss Eck discussing mine. They were standing facing each other talking about my test. I knew because they looked over at me a couple of times. They both had huge chests and they were standing kind of far apart so their chests wouldn't bounce off each other.

They looked like two huge robins discussing a worm.

There was a lot of sighing and then they came and

told me that I'd have to do the test again the next day. By the looks on their faces I figured they were saying that they knew I was stupid, sure, but could I possibly be that stupid? Could I be something subhuman? You'd have to be in a coma or something to score that low.

But Dad said that maybe I scored so high that the test couldn't record it—maybe I blew out all the tubes in the thing and they figured only a genius could score that high and they figured something went wrong with their test because even Albert Einstein couldn't score that high.

And they say he invented the atomic bomb.

That made me feel a little better.

But I didn't really blame Miss Strong for laughing when I said I wanted to be a writer.

After all, I was the second worst writer in the class.

Melody Bleach was the worst writer in the class. Her main problem was she never had a pencil and she couldn't write with a pen and a nib because she pressed too hard.

Dad said the reason was, she wasn't organized.

And she always put her tongue out when she tried to write after she borrowed a pencil or the teacher gave her one.

She'd stick her tongue between her teeth when she was trying to think of what to write. Some of the kids would laugh at her and make fun of her.

I laughed at her too but I also felt sort of sorry for her.

Specially when she wet herself. That was in Grade Three, I think. Melody wet herself. She was too scared of Miss Frack or Miss Eck, or whoever it was, to ask if she could leave the room.

So she just sat there and the water ran down off the seat into a pool on the floor under her desk. And the water ran down her cheeks from her eyes. There was water running out of her from both ends.

I think Dad was right. Her main problem was that she wasn't organized. Dad always says, get organized and you can't go wrong.

I was sitting there worrying about Sammy's father when suddenly I heard Blue Cheeks saying my name. Everybody was looking over at me. Even Margot. And Blue Cheeks was getting bluer. He was asking me about a grammar sentence. He was writing on the blackboard but he was looking at me.

Blue Cheeks could turn his head *right* around without moving his body. His head would start turning slowly and it would keep turning and turning until it was facing the other way. Then it would start back until it was back almost to the same spot. He could turn his head left and right so far that he could cover the whole 360 degrees without moving his shoulders. His head must have been on a swivel or something.

He would write grammar sentences on the board so that we could copy them out and then tell him what was wrong with them.

All the sentences he ever wrote on the board were wrong.

Every day we wrote down hundreds of sentences that were wrong.

Some of them were quite funny but if he heard anybody laughing or snorting, old Blue Cheeks's head would start coming around, slowly, slowly. And we'd all sit there, hypnotized by how far his head could come round.

I used to think it would unscrew and tumble right off onto the floor.

But then, of course, if that happened he could catch it just before it hit because his hands hung down there near the floor anyway.

Somebody must have coughed or something and he looked around and couldn't catch anybody so he noticed I was in a trance and picked me as his victim.

I was thinking about Sammy's father, so I must have been staring into the blackboard like I was hypnotized. Dad said later that I must have looked like a cow watching a train go by.

"You! What is wrong with this sentence?"

He was pointing at the sentence he had just written on the board.

"Read the sentence, please," he said.

I read it. "Ralph edged closer as the moose sniffed suspiciously and snapped the picture," the sentence said.

"Well?" said Blue Cheeks.

I looked at the sentence again.

"Tell us, Mr. Daydreams, what is wrong with this sentence."

"It's something to do with the camera," I said.

"It's something to do with the camera, is it?" His head was right around facing me full-on now and his shoulders were still facing the blackboard. It seemed impossible.

"And the moose," I said, "and something to do with the moose."

"The camera and the moose," said Blue Cheeks, sarcasm dripping off his lips like syrup.

"And Ralph," I said, just to make sure, "there's something wrong with Ralph too."

"And what do you suppose it is that is wrong with Ralph?" said Blue Cheeks.

"He hasn't got the camera," I said.

"And who has the camera?"

"The moose seems to have the camera."

"And why has the moose got the camera instead of Ralph?"

"I don't know, sir. It seems strange, a moose with a camera."

"Why has the moose got the camera?"

"Maybe he took it from Ralph?"

"Why hasn't Ralph got his own camera?" Blue Cheeks's face was dark blue now.

"Maybe it *isn't* Ralph's camera!" I said, thinking I was on to something. "Maybe Ralph hasn't got a camera and the moose has a camera and Ralph's sneaking up on the moose to steal his camera!"

"Read the sentence again!"

"Ralph edged closer as the moose sniffed suspiciously and snapped the picture." I almost knew it off by heart by now.

"What is wrong with that sentence?"

Behind me sat Geranium Mayburger, the dumbest girl in the school. Geranium loved to whisper answers to people. Specially people in trouble.

"Hooves," she whispered behind me. "A moose can't take a picture because his hooves are too big for the button."

"Five seconds," said Blue Cheeks, "or you stay and write lines!" He sounded like he was choking. I was desperate.

"A moose could never hold a camera properly or snap a picture because of its large and clumsy hooves," I said, trying to make the best sentence I could.

I knew I was doomed, so I sat down.

Blue Cheeks gurgled, "One hundred lines—'I must learn my grammar!'"

A few minutes later the bell rang for recess and I was suddenly alone.

I had specially wanted to get out this recess and find CoCo Laframboise (nephew of Toe-Jam) on Angel Square and ask him what he thought of what happened to Sammy's father. CoCo is my best Pea Soup friend. He goes to Brother Brébeuf and their recess is the same time as ours. CoCo is smart and he is a good detective. He would be out there right now, fighting away, having a great time.

And I was stuck in here.

I wrote my lines like I always did, holding three pencils in my fingers so three lines would get written at once. I was the best line-writer in the class. I was so good and so fast, sometimes people would pay me to write their lines for them. I charged seven cents a hundred.

When I was finished I had time to write down what I had to get done before Christmas Day, which was exactly one week away.

1. Worry about what happened to Sammy's father.
2. See the eclipse of the moon tonight.
3. Get presents for Aunt Dottie, Dad, my sister Pamela, my friends and maybe one other, very special present.
4. Go to the show.
5. Work at home on the ashes.
6. Work at Talmud Torah.
7. Work at Woolworth's.
8. Be altar boy at St. Brigit's Dogan Church.
9. Sing at St. Albany's Protestant Church.
10. Get the lovely Margot Lane to notice me.

At noon I raced across Angel Square to go home for dinner.

On the square the war was raging.

I could see Killer Bodnoff, who, last year, was the toughest Jew, and my friend CoCo Laframboise, who was busy being the toughest Pea Soup; Manfred Mahoney, who was the toughest Dogan; not Denny Trail, the toughest Protestant, who had moved to New Edinburgh; Arnold Levinson, who was the sissiest Jew; Telesphore Bourgignon, who was the sissiest Pea Soup; Clary O'Mara, who was the sissiest Dogan; not Sherwood Ashbury, the sissiest Protestant, who had moved to Bank Street somewhere; Anita Pleet, who was the smartest girl; Martha Banting, who was the nicest girl; Geranium Mayburger, who was the dumbest girl; Fleurette Featherstone Fitchell, who was the dirtiest girl, even dirtier than Delbert Dilabio, and he was the dirtiest guy in Lowertown.

And Margot Lane, walking beautifully home to Whitepath Street.

And I was Lamont Cranston, invisible for now, racing home across Angel Square.

I don't know why, but as I was losing one small fight I was remembering something that happened with Fleurette Featherstone Fitchell in my laneway one time.

She drew an oval in the dirt with a stick. Then she cut it in half with another line. It looked like the side view of a hamburger bun.

She asked me if I knew what it was.

"It's a hamburger bun from the side," I said.

"No it isn't, silly!" she said. "It's something I've got that you haven't got." Then she drew what looked like a cigar in the dirt with her stick.

"Guess what that is," she said.

"A cigar," I said.

"No it isn't, silly!" she said.

Then she asked me if I wanted to see hers.

Our laneway is between two brick walls. The brick starts part way up and there is cement on the lower part. It is on the smooth lower part that we play alleys off the wall. In the summer the ground is mostly dirt with some weeds here and there. There are quite a few holes that have been dug for playing alleys and there are some shiny bits of glass around. And some small stones. When it rains there is a strong smell of cat piss.

I said no.

On the square, Delbert Dilabio and some guys were standing around saying things and listening to Fleurette Featherstone Fitchell saying worse things right back to them.

Killer Bodnoff and CoCo Laframboise were in a death grip in the corner of the yard.

Manfred Mahoney was looking for Denny Trail.

Anita Pleet was trying to explain something to Geranium Mayburger.

I left the square, ran up Papineau and down Cobourg to my house. I waved at my sister Pamela in her window and went in. Aunt Dottie gave me soup and peanut butter and homemade biscuits while we listened to "Big Sister" on the radio at twelve-fifteen. It was the same as yesterday. They were still arguing about whether Big Sister's sister should marry some soldier from somewhere. Halfway through the "Farm Broadcast" at twelve-thirty the radio tubes faded out again and I didn't hear a thing until the one o'clock signal came on.

At the sound of the long dash I left, while Aunt Dottie was reminding me about changing into my old breeks from my good breeks right after school before I went out again.

On the way back across Angel Square I had a chance to talk to CoCo, who wasn't too busy. He had just one guy down in the snow, throttling him with his own scarf. He'd let the scarf go loose a little and make the guy sing parts of this stupid song that was on the radio all the time.

Chickory Chick
Cha-la cha-la
Check a la romey in a
Bannana-ka
Wallika wallika
Can't you see?
Chickory chick
Is me!

We talked about Sammy's father.

"Maybe he's took somebody's job," CoCo said after

we talked for a while between bits of "Chickory Chick." CoCo thought that maybe somebody was mad because Sammy's father got the job as night watchman and somebody else didn't and so they went and beat him up.

In a bannana-ka
Wallika wallika
Can't you see…?

said the guy being choked under the snow.

"He don't know dis song very good, eh Lamont?" commented CoCo.

"What about the Ritchie's Feed and Seed bag?" I said as CoCo tightened the scarf up a notch and the singer went quiet.

"Maybe somebody from da store," said CoCo, my favorite detective. "Somebody from da store who hates Jews."

Maybe he was right. It could have been somebody at the feed store. Would they be that dumb, though? Wearing a mask with the name written all over it? Maybe.

The five-minute bell rang at York Street School. I had to go. I said thanks and goodbye to CoCo.

"See you, Lamont," CoCo said, going back to his work on the singer. "'Ow's da lovely Margot Lane?"

"I'm going to buy her a Christmas present," I said.

"Bonne idée," called out CoCo, and I saw him start to pack his victim's mouth full of snow.

That afternoon we had science and our teacher, Mr.

Maynard, was telling us again about the eclipse and how the earth stands between the sun and the moon and blocks out the light. And how you can see the shadow of the earth crossing the moon until the moon is completely dark.

Mr. Maynard, for homework, told us to watch it from nine o'clock to nine-thirty. The complete eclipse would be at exactly nine-twenty.

Killer Bodnoff said he could stay up all right but he couldn't watch the eclipse because "Gangbusters" was on the radio at nine.

Arnold Levinson said he'd try to watch it but he didn't know if he could last because he gets awful tired and anyway he's afraid of the dark.

Anita Pleet could watch it, yes, and as a matter of fact she had her own telescope and she'd do a project on it for Mr. Maynard if he'd like.

Martha Banting couldn't stay up because she was too nice.

Geranium Mayburger wanted to know where this whole thing was going to take place and would it be on her street too.

Fleurette Featherstone Fitchell asked all the boys in the seats around her if they wanted to come over and watch it in her back shed.

I said I could stay up and watch it.

Margot Lane said she would stay up and watch it from her bedroom window.

Then Mr. Maynard said a beautiful thing about the moon. He said this: "The lunar surface is fixed and unchanging while the Earth changes with each day, month and season. Let a single leaf fall from a tree on Earth and there will have been a greater change than may occur on the moon in a hundred autumns."

Mr. Maynard was the best teacher I ever had.

On my way home from school things were fairly quiet on the square and I only had one fight. I had some extra time so I cut up Heney Street and went into Sammy's place in the apartments beside the car barns.

I knocked on the door three or four times but nobody answered.

Then a lady came down the hall and told me that Sammy and his mother went to Toronto because Sammy's father had been taken there to a better hospital where he could have an operation on his head.

It was pretty serious.

After she went back down the hall I stood there for a while by myself and had a little conversation with Sammy's door.

"I lost one of my fights today because you weren't here, Sammy."

No answer, of course.

"Two Pea Soups jumped me from the rear on Angel Square. You weren't there in your usual lookout position."

The door didn't say a word.

"Who did this to your dad, Sammy? You don't know,

do you? The only clues we have are that he was wearing that mask-bag with the seed store writing on it and that he hates Jews. That's all we know."

A silent, lonesome door.

"I'm going to get CoCo and Gerald to help me find out who did it."

I left Sammy's, passed by the car barns, and went home.

At my house I waved at my sister Pamela in her window. As soon as I got in the door she rushed to me and gave me a big squeeze. She always did that.

After Aunt Dottie inspected me I changed out of my good breeks and went down the cellar to shake the ashes. Our furnace burns wood and coal. You shake the furnace. Not the whole furnace (I used to think when Dad went down he'd put his big arms right around the red-hot furnace with all the octopus pipes crawling out over his head and he'd get really red in the face and he'd give the whole furnace a big shake, he was so strong) but just the grates of the furnace by attaching a crank handle to a steel rod and turning it (I used to pretend I was starting a car) and making the grate turn and the ashes fall into the bottom.

Then you shovel the ashes into the sifter and sift them because sometimes some coal that isn't burnt yet falls through and you have to pick those pieces off the screen and put them back in the furnace because coal is expensive.

The sifter is a kind of tub with rockers on the bottom and two handles and a screen and a lid. You grab it by the handles and shake it and rock it.

And the dust flies up into your face and chokes you.

Dad gave Aunt Dottie one for Christmas two years ago.

The furnace can be dangerous because if the coal is just starting to burn it makes poisonous gas, so you have to open up the drafts and make the gas go up the chimney instead of up the pipes and into your rooms where it will kill you.

Aunt Dottie often says "I smell gas" and runs down the cellar with her rubber apron on and opens up the drafts and lets all the expensive heat out over the low, small roofs of Lowertown.

"I don't smell gas," Dad said once when Aunt Dottie ran down the cellar. "She probably just let a little poop."

And I laughed for about twelve days every time I thought about what he said.

I laughed in school and everybody turned around and Blue Cheeks swung his eyes around onto me just like he was a searchlight at a prison looking for the escaping convict.

And people at recess would say I was crazy, laughing for nothing. And people on the streetcar when I would be going uptown would look over at me and shake their heads: imagine, a boy so young, and crazy already. "It must be the war," I heard one lady say to another.

"Maybe it's germs," I said under my breath and I started laughing all over again.

And here I was, shaking the ashes (I got ten cents each time for doing it) and thinking that Christmas was getting close but I didn't have any Christmas feeling yet. I was wondering when it was going to come. You couldn't make it come. It had to just happen.

But it better happen soon, I thought. Time was going on.

After supper at eight o'clock I listened to "Big Town" with Dad while Aunt Dottie put my sister on her rubber sheet with the talcum powder.

"Big Town," with Steve Wilson of the Illustrated Press and his secretary, the lovely Loreli Kilbourne.

At nine o'clock I got bundled up and went out into the beautiful clear and cold Lowertown winter night and looked up at the full moon.

The shadow of the earth was part way over it, taking a curved bite out of the side.

I could imagine standing there on the moon with this big smooth shadow coming over me. On the moon where nothing ever happens.

One leaf falls, Mr. Maynard said. A big event.

It was so peaceful I started to cry.

The shadow of my Earth moved slowly over the smooth moon.

If you looked right at it, you couldn't see it move but if you looked beside it, you could.

Soon it was completely covered. There was just a furry glow around the outside. Like the frost around my sister's face in her window.

I stood there on Cobourg Street for a while and watched some clouds blow over. I could sniff snow.

Then I could feel the Christmas feeling coming. It was coming over me. Coming up in me. Filling me up.

A feeling of bells and chocolate, hymns and carols, beautiful cold winter and warm rooms. Windows with snow and berries. And laughing and hugging.

In a little while it started to snow.

Big fat flakes.

Every one a big event, Mr. Maynard.

I turned around and went in the house and to bed, plotting about how to solve the mystery of Sammy's dad and letting Christmas come in and out.

2 Cul de Dead End

SIR JOHN A. MACDONALD was Canada's first prime minister. His birthday is on January 11. Last January when Margot Lane first came to our school (she wasn't in my class) I sent her a card. The card said: "Happy Sir John A. Macdonald's Birthday!" I signed it: "The Shadow."

I saw her every day in the schoolyard or on Angel Square but she never ran up to me and said thanks for the lovely card.

In February I sent her a card on Groundhog Day, Valentine's Day and Ash Wednesday.

That didn't do any good so in March she got a St. David's Day card, a St. Patrick's Day card and a First Day of Spring card from "Lamont Cranston, The Shadow." Some of the cards I made myself and some I bought.

In April she got an Easter card and a St. George's Day

card. In May a Mother's Day and a Victoria Day. In June Lamont sent her a Father's Day card and a First Day of Summer card.

From up at Low in July she got a Happy July card and in August a Congratulations on the Opening of the Ottawa Exhibition card.

When school started back in September (she was in my class now) I sent her a Yom Kippur card. In October a Thanksgiving card and a Halloween card. In November an All Saints' Day card and a St. Andrew's Day card.

Now it was December. It was almost a whole year since my first card and she still hadn't run up to me and said thanks for the lovely card. This month it was going to be a present. Not a card.

If that didn't work, I was going to give up.

CoCo Laframboise, my best Pea Soup friend, knew. Sammy, my best Jew friend, knew. Gerald, my best Dogan friend, knew. They also knew I couldn't just go up to her and tell her that I was Lamont Cranston, The Shadow, and that I was sending her all those cards. It would be too foolish. She would have to find out. She would have to want to find out on her own.

Gerald and Delbert Dilabio were standing outside my house when I came out the next morning to go to school. Delbert went to St. Brigit's of the Bleeding Thorns with my friend Gerald. I didn't like Delbert. And I had a good reason.

Delbert used to keep a frozen horseball or two in his hat in case of ambush. He surprised a lot of Jews and Pea Soups with those.

Gerald told me that when Father Francis came around to check Delbert's homework you could tell that Father didn't think that Delbert's head smelled very good. Lucky for Father, Gerald said, that he had very long arms. He could use his long arm to mark Delbert's homework all wrong while keeping his nose way up in the air near the ceiling.

But that wasn't why I didn't like Delbert.

Cobourg Street was pretty empty. Tons of snow floating down.

Just the odd streetcar going home to the barns.

I waved at my sister Pamela in her window.

"What does your sister think about?" Delbert said, as he packed a particularly big horse-snow-ball.

"I don't know what she thinks about," I said. "I know what she likes, though. She likes feeling Hello and she hates feeling Goodbye. When I come home she grabs me and hugs me so tight I can hardly breathe. She's pretty strong. Even if I just go to the store and come right back she hugs me like that. Just like I'd been gone for two years or something."

A streetcar came up Cobourg Street in a slow, quiet way. Around Christmas they were always like that. The snow made everything quiet. You'd just suddenly see one. Not like in the summer. In the summer you could hear them coming even before they turned onto Cobourg from St. Patrick.

We waved at the driver.

"This is what she thinks about. She thinks about Hello and Good-bye. The milkman and the breadman and the mailman get hugged pretty good too if they come in the door too far."

Cobourg Street was silent.

"What's wrong with her?" said Delbert.

"She's M.D.," Gerald said. Gerald knew nearly everything about my sister.

I didn't mind telling Delbert what he wanted to know. Even though he was so dirty. The more people who knew, the better.

And safer.

"What's M.D.?" Delbert asked.

"Mentally Deficient," I said. "She was born that way. Every time I go out the door she starts howling and crying a bit. Then she runs to her window and I wave at her and then she's all right."

"How old is she?" said Delbert.

"Two years older than me."

"Why doesn't she come out?"

"Can't," I said.

"Why?"

"Aunt Dottie can't let her out."

"Why?"

"Because she'd get lost," Gerald said.

"She used to be out in the summer," Delbert said. "I saw her."

"Yeah. Tied up so she wouldn't go away or get knocked down by a streetcar or something."

"Why can't she come out on her rope in the winter?"

"Has to have somebody guard her now."

"Why?"

"Because last summer some boys pulled her pants down. Didn't you know that?" I looked right into Delbert Dilabio's face.

"Who did?" said Gerald. He had mad in his voice.

"Arnie Sultzburger and some guys," I said, looking right at Delbert.

"What happened?"

"Aunt Dottie went out and slapped his face. Then Dad went over to Arnie's place and told Mr. Sultzburger that if Arnie ever came around here again he would kill him. That's the only time I ever saw Dad mad."

"Good," said Gerald. "That's good. I think I'll kill Arnie the next time I see him."

A Bourque's ice truck came down Cobourg Street in the quiet snow.

"She still wets the bed, you know. She wears napkins. She's like a little baby," I said. "I guess she's just like a little baby. Wave at her."

I knew Delbert had been with Arnie when that happened. And now Gerald knew too. I could tell by the look on his face.

Things would be a lot safer for my sister now. Gerald would help see to that.

Gerald said he'd walk part way over Angel Square with me since I didn't have Sammy. Three-quarters of the way over the square he would turn right and go to Bleeding Thorns and then I'd meet CoCo and he'd walk the rest of the way with me before he turned left to go to Brother Brébeuf. Then I didn't have far to go to York.

Gerald and I went down Papineau and onto the square. Because Gerald is a Dogan we'd only have to fight Jews and Pea Soups. If I was with Sammy I'd only have to fight Dogans and Pea Soups. If I was with CoCo I'd only have to fight Jews and Dogans. If I was with Sammy, CoCo and Gerald I wouldn't have to fight anybody.

And if I was alone…

Well, you know what would happen then.

I'd have to fight everybody.

Because I'm not anything.

While Gerald and I were strangling two Pea Soups with their own scarves, we were discussing the mystery of Sammy's father.

"Two clues," Gerald was saying as his Pea Soup's eyes started to bulge out pretty far, "two clues. He hates Jews and he has something to do with Ritchie's Feed and Seed."

"There are hundreds of people around here who hate Jews," I said as I released my Pea Soup's scarf a bit to give him a chance to breathe a couple of times because his face was getting a kind of purple color.

"Well," said Gerald as his Pea Soup started to gurgle, "let's start with the feed and seed store."

"Right," I said. "We'll go today at lunch time. See what we can see."

"Get CoCo to come," said Gerald as he let his Pea Soup beg for mercy for a while before burying him in the snow.

"Good idea," I said.

After Gerald turned right to go to Bleeding Thorns, CoCo and I took on a small group of Dogans who didn't put up much of a fight. One of them had a yoyo with him and CoCo shoved it in his mouth to see if he could swallow it.

The two Jews we had to do were quite a bit tougher.

"Gerald thinks we should go to the seed store to check things out," I said to CoCo as my Jew tried to bite my ear off.

"Bonne idée," CoCo said as he tore the back out of his Jew's coat.

"Can you come with us at lunch time?" I said.

"Sure ting," CoCo said. "We can see if anybody dere 'ates Jews."

"We'll meet you on the corner of Friel and York," I said as my Jew ripped off my galosh and whipped me with it.

"See you dere," CoCo said.

The bell rang and our fight ended in a draw.

For some reason thinking about going to the feed store got my Christmas spirit back, so during Blue Cheeks's grammar class I figured out my shopping money.

The sentence we were supposed to be working on was this one: "I gave him a friendly slap as he left the room on his back."

I worked on my money instead.

Money Saved So Far

Shaking Ashes fifteen times —	1.50
Writing Lines for Killer Bodnoff, Fleurette Featherstone Fitchell and Geranium Mayburger —	.21
Waxing Floors three times at Talmud Torah —	1.50
Singing Choir four Sundays at St. Albany's Church —	2.00
Altar Boying one funeral, one wedding at St. Brigit's Church —	1.00
Working two After-Schools at Woolworth's —	1.40
Four weeks' allowance —	1.00
Total So Far —	$8.61

"Well, Mr. Daydreams," I heard Blue Cheeks saying, "do we know the answer today?"

"The words 'on his back' are in the wrong place," I said without looking up from my expense sheets.

"It should say, 'I gave him a friendly slap on the back as he left the room'."

Those wrong sentences were a lot easier if you didn't think about them.

I looked up and Blue Cheeks was staring at me with hatred in his face. He hated it when you got something right.

What a teacher.

That afternoon in Mr. Maynard's class we discussed the eclipse.

Killer Bodnoff said that last night on "Gangbusters" the moon was mentioned. Some crooks were stealing furs from a warehouse and the moon came out and the G-men shot all the crooks in the head.

Arnold Levinson said he was in bed with his eyes shut but he thought he *heard* the eclipse.

Anita Pleet had a huge project already finished, which she presented to Mr. Maynard with pictures pasted on it and printing and arrows explaining the whole thing. She said she read that a day on the moon was 708 hours long.

Martha Banting said, "Mr. Maynard, would you ever be *tired* after a long day like *that*, *wouldn't* you, Mr. Maynard!" She was so nice.

Geranium Mayburger said she couldn't find the eclipse.

Fleurette Featherstone Fitchell said she was discussing the eclipse in her back shed with some boys and by the time they let her out it was over.

I said that it reminded me of Christmas and then I felt kind of stupid for saying it.

Margot Lane said she watched it from her window and saw the whole thing. She said it made her think of all the other people around Lowertown who were probably watching it too. She said she was imagining what some of the other people in the class were thinking about when they were watching the same thing she was watching.

Or something like that.

Then she looked across the class at me.

At least I thought it was me.

Mr. Maynard had hung up some balsam and spruce and pine branches around the room.

It made the room smell like Christmas. The feeling was getting easy.

At lunch time I met CoCo and Gerald and we headed up York Street to the By Ward Market. Outside Devine's store there was a lot of activity. Sleighs piled with wreaths and branches and near them some stands with mistletoe and painted clumps of berries. And ladies selling cranberries. And Toe-Jam Laframboise loading up his delivery truck.

We went by R. Hector Aubrey's and there was a big crowd outside talking about the No Turkeys sign he had in the window.

We went into Ritchie's Feed and Seed store. Every bag in the store had those words printed on it. Everybody in the store was carrying one of those bags. Everybody leaving the store had one of those bags with those words.

"It's hopeless," Gerald said. "Everybody's got these bags."

"Maybe somebody who works at dis place 'ates Jews," CoCo said.

"Let's try to find out," I said and we moved deeper into the store, past the wire fencing and the fertilizer and the milk pails and the gardening tools.

Farther back in the store we could hear what sounded like an argument. I recognized Mr. Slipacoff, who owned the kosher butcher shop down the street, talking very loud to Mr. Ritchie in front of the seed counter.

CoCo and Gerald and I hid behind some sacks of feed and listened. After a while we could tell they weren't arguing. They were telling jokes and laughing. Then Mr. Slipacoff gave Mr. Ritchie a bag of fat meat and suet and they weighed it and had a pretend argument and then Mr. Ritchie weighed up a bag of broken seed bits and they traded the suet for the seeds.

And then they laughed and Mr. Ritchie pulled out a bottle from under the counter and they both had a drink and laughed and hugged each other and sang a little Pea Soup song about chickadees being a Canadian winter bird and Mr. Aubrey came in the back door in his bloody apron and Mr. Devine came in and they all had another drink or two and traded biscuits and suet and seeds and laughed and danced around.

"Here's to the chickadee! May he eat in the winter in

peace, now that the war is over!" said Mr. Ritchie and they started telling jokes again.

They were trading food for their bird feeders.

"And it's your turn in the spring," said Mr. Devine, "to have the party!" He was talking to Mr. Slipacoff. "I'll bring the syrup. We'll have our hummingbird party!"

CoCo and Gerald and I were watching their bird party. Happy men. They didn't hate each other.

"What are you kids doing there?" Mr. Ritchie said, noticing us behind the bags.

"Nothing," I said, standing up, embarrassed. "We're doing a school project on birds."

The men all laughed and gave us some suet and broken biscuits and seeds for our birds and we went out of the store feeling very silly.

"Hopeless," Gerald said. "Nobody here hates anybody."

"A cul de dead end," said CoCo as we divided up the bird food and went back to Angel Square.

After school CoCo helped me across Angel Square and I ducked into Sammy's apartment to see if he was there yet. He wasn't, so I went home and changed my good breeks and took off to my job at Talmud Torah.

Talmud Torah is at 171 George Street back near the market. There are eleven wide wooden steps and solid wide wooden railings and two white pillars and two wooden paneled doors and a stone archway.

There are two windows, one on each side of the stairs.

There are white kitchen curtains on the windows and a Star of David in each. The sign beside the doors says in English: Ottawa Talmud Torah. And underneath on the sign is some writing in Hebrew.

I felt the Hebrew writing with my fingers like I always did, trying to understand it.

The writing is like curly hairs, crooked wires, dots and half snowmen.

I felt the mystery with my fingers.

I tried to whisper the mystery but I couldn't.

Inside, I piled up the chairs of the schoolroom, swept the old hardwood floor, spread on the paste wax, polished the floor with the big mop with the cinder block on it for weight, and put the chairs back.

While I was doing that I looked at all the photographs around the walls of men with long beards and women in black dresses and groups of kids with their little caps and tried to read the curly hairs and crooked wires and dots and half snowmen written on the blackboard.

And I thought a lot about Sammy and his father.

It was a mystery.

That night at supper Aunt Dottie and Dad had a little argument about whether you call it supper or dinner.

Dad said they could compromise and call it "dipper" or maybe even "sunner" and Aunt Dottie said he was just being silly and that it was nothing to joke about.

Then Dad changed the subject and told us he couldn't get a turkey for Christmas because there was still a shortage of turkeys because of the war and Aunt Dottie said he should get two chickens instead.

"Yes," Dad said, "that sounds all right. We could have two nice chickens for Christmas dipper."

"Dinner," Aunt Dottie said.

"Sunner," Dad said.

"Why are there chickens but no turkeys?" I said.

"Because of the war," Aunt Dottie said.

"But why?" I said.

"Because they used them all in the war," Dad said.

"Don't listen to him," Aunt Dottie said.

"What did they use them for?" I said.

"They dropped them out of airplanes onto the Germans," Dad said.

"Lies," Aunt Dottie said.

"They also used them as camouflage."

"Why do you fill the boy's mind with lies?" Aunt Dottie said.

"They were also sent in as spies—espionage."

"Don't listen to him," Aunt Dottie said, and she covered up my ears.

At nine-thirty I listened to "The Shadow" with my head under the radio. Me and the cat.

The lovely Margot Lane was in a cave with a ghoul and Lamont Cranston turned into The Shadow and saved her.

The cat purred as The Shadow laughed and said "Crime does not pay!" and the organ got stabbed.

And I wondered if it was me she was looking at across the classroom when she said those things about the eclipse.

My Margot Lane. The real Margot Lane.

3 Just a Comic

THE NEXT MORNING, while I was standing on the heat getting ready to do Angel Square again without Sammy, the breadman opened the door and came in. He had Morrison-Lamothe on his cap and his basket was hooked over his arm. My sister Pamela nearly knocked him over giving him his hug. He smelled like horses and bread and cold winter air.

In his basket he had Christmas-wrapped cake and doughnuts and boxes with ribbons around them and jelly rolls with Santa stickers on them in crinkly transparent paper and gingersnaps that would be snappy even if it was a summer day. Gingersnaps in a row like huge brown pennies in long narrow boxes. And Aunt Dottie bought some gingersnaps and bread and Morrison-Lamothe smiled and gave her two small gingersnaps change (they were pennies this time) and (though it was pretty early) she gave him his little Christmas present all neatly wrapped and stuck. I knew it would take him hours to get it open once he got home.

Then my sister Pamela gave Morrison-Lamothe and me another big hug and I left for school.

On the way down Papineau, Gerald and I had a little talk with Chalmers Lonnigan, the Dogan who believed that God made the sidewalks and the streetcars and that Jews and Pea Soups went to hell when they died.

Gerald specially liked talking to Chalmers because of the crazy things he'd say.

"Aren't Pea Soups Dogans, Chalmers?" Gerald said.

"No they ain't. They're Pea Soups!" Chalmers said.

"Are Jews Pea Soups?" I said.

"No," said Chalmers, "they're Jews. They go to hell. And God made the streetcar tracks."

Gerald and I took turns talking to him, asking him things.

"What do Jews and Pea Soups do in hell when they get there?"

"They lie around with their tongues stuck to the streetcar tracks."

"Why?"

"Because they're Jews and Pea Soups."

"What happens to Dogans after they die?

"Oh, they go to heaven."

"What do they do in heaven when they get there?"

"They eat pie and sing."

"What else?"

"Sometimes they get to go to the show. And you get a new cap gun whenever you want. And even a new bicycle maybe. And you don't have to take a bath unless you want to. And every week a man comes around and gives you ten dollars."

"Ten dollars! What for?"

"For candy, I guess."

"Is that heaven?"

"I guess so," said Chalmers, with a kind of sad look on his face. "I can't wait to go."

There was a long pause while we stood there listening to the snow fall down. Chalmers was thinking.

"Chalmers," I said. "What are you doing now?"

"Thinking," said Chalmers.

"What are you thinking about?"

"The atomic bomb," Chalmers said.

"The atomic bomb?" I said.

"What is the atomic bomb?" Chalmers asked, still looking down between his feet.

Gerald started telling Chalmers about the atomic bomb. He told him it was quite a small bomb but it could kill everybody in the world.

"The atomic bomb could kill everybody in the world!" I said.

"So?" said Chalmers.

"It's not like ordinary bombs that blow up buildings and factories and trains and hospitals and stuff," I said.

"This is a little wee bomb about the size of a pea, I think, and it blows up everything and kills everybody!"

"So?" Chalmers said.

"And anybody who's left gets sick and swells up for about a month and bursts."

"So?"

"Think of it this way," Gerald said. "What if I told you that there was one of these bombs on its way down on us right now. What would you say?"

"I dunno."

"Okay Chalmers, there's one of those atomic bombs falling right down towards us right now, and when it hits here, everything is going to get blown up—everything—and everybody's going to be burnt to death and die!"

"Would it get all the Jews?"

"Remember last summer when they dropped one on the Japs and blew up Japan? Do you remember that, Chalmers?"

There was a long pause. The snow was piled up so high you couldn't see across the street. People would come down the sidewalk and go in their laneways and disappear, the snow was so high. The steel rungs up the wooden telephone poles were each stacked with snow. The wires were loaded with snow. The window sills were piled with snow. Every twig and branch of every tree was weighed down with snow. The sparrows and chickadees had to shovel little spaces for themselves so they could sit on the fences, there was so much snow. The cats were under the verandahs and steps, peeking out, crabby looks on their faces, wondering what to do about all the snow.

"I wish I was a Jap," said Chalmers.

"You're not very organized, Chalmers," I said. "You should try to get organized."

"If I was a Jap, I'd be dead now, because of the bomb, and I'd be in heaven. Heaven is nicer than Papineau, you know," said Chalmers.

Gerald and I looked at each other. Chalmers had never sounded like this before.

Then he said some more.

"My father says every time you see a Jew you should hit him and try to kill him!"

"Your father's crazy," I said.

After a few fights, Gerald and I met CoCo and we had a meeting.

CoCo said not to give up just because the feed store was a dead end. He said we should go to the car barns, the scene of the crime, and see what we could see.

After school I went right to my job at Woolworth's on Rideau Street.

Woolworth's. A Christmas madhouse. Perfume and candy and squeaky wooden floors. Records playing. The smell of perfume and chocolates mixed. Salesgirls with lipstick and earrings and long, curly hair. And pictures of Santa Claus everywhere. Long red and silver fuzzy streamers swinging and arching over the aisles. Wind-up trucks crackling away and the smell of hot dogs and fried eggs at the lunch counter. And toast. And the smell of damp fur and wet cloth and wet leather, the snow on people's clothes melting in Woolworth's. And people at the doors stamping their feet. The salesgirls and saleswomen laughing and talking to the people and to each other and the salesgirls' earrings sparkling and their long, curly hair bouncing and swinging over the perfume and around the chocolates and the toys and the toast and the pictures of Santa Claus.

Santa Clauses all over. Big ones hanging, laughing fat-faced, bulging eyes, big black boots, one foot up on a fake sleigh loaded with wrapped parcels of all sizes and shapes; smaller Santas standing on counters, holding radios or pointing at record players; Santas peeking out of mirrors, smiling and wishing everybody Merry Christmas; Santa being kissed by a beautiful movie star because of a dish of ice cream; Santa pasted on the walls eating chocolates; Santa, standing in the corner, peeking at people opening perfume; Santa modeling socks; Santa saying go to church; Santas sprayed on glass counters; Santas hanging and turning on threads; a record, somewhere, of Santa laughing and bells jingling; Salvation Army Santa, just outside the door, kicking his own boots, jangling his bells and hiding somewhere in clouds of his own breath, small icicles stiffening his white beard.

Red paper bells hanging from the lights making no sound at all.

And thousands of people carrying parcels and bags and dragging kids.

Dragging kids to go up and talk to the inside Santa on his throne.

It was Ozzie O'Driscoll again. Ozzie was a policeman who'd take his holidays around Christmas and get a part-time job playing Santa at Woolworth's. He used to pinch the kids and tickle them in the face with his beard and tell them a whole lot of stuff they never heard before about the North Pole. Like how Mrs. Claus used to hit him over the head with frying pans and pots if he didn't remember to bring every little kid in the world whatever he wanted. And he'd get them to feel the lumps on his head where she got him with a pan or a pot. And he'd tell them how sick he'd be after making his rounds and eating all that stuff everybody left out for him. Or how he could never remember the names of his reindeer and could they suggest some better names, names easier to remember. And some of the kids who weren't as shy as the others would suggest names like Uncle Jim or Captain Marvel for Santa's reindeer instead of Donner and Blitzen and those others. And often the kids would get so interested they'd forget to tell him what they wanted for Christmas and you'd see them going away afterwards with their parents trying to explain what happened.

Sometimes a parent would stop in the middle of the store and there'd be a little argument with the kid maybe, and maybe they'd both look back at Ozzie O'Driscoll, special Santa, at Woolworth's on Rideau.

My job at Woolworth's was bringing up stuff from the basement and putting it on the shelves. I'd come by Santa O'Driscoll each time, carrying the stuff. He'd always give me a big wink. You could almost believe in him, he was so good.

I wanted to go and ask him what to do about solving the crime. But I didn't. I felt silly about it. Maybe when I had at least a clue, then I could talk to him about it.

After supper Gerald and CoCo and I went up to the car barns to look around. The snow outside was black with grease from the streetcars. There are ten tracks leading into the blackness of the barns. Each entrance holds ten streetcars. When all the cars are in, sitting over the hundred grease pits, there are thousands of places to hide.

We slipped into Entrance Five between the cars, ran down the row and went carefully down the five slippery cement stairs into one of the pits and turned on the working light.

Looking up under the streetcar into the wheels and springs and steel, we could feel the weight above us. The grease and dust mixed under our feet into a soft mat. There were wrenches and bars lying around and heavy metal braces. Anything like this could be used for hitting a person over the head.

Suddenly we heard the new night watchman punch his time clock down the row and we switched out the light and stood flat against the wall of the pit, our heads almost touching the wheels of the streetcar above us. We heard him coming down the row, whistling softly to himself a little Christmas carol and soon his light flashed in our pit and out and over to the next one. Then he stopped whistling. He was listening.

We stopped breathing.

Then we heard some giggling and someone saying, "Sh!"

"Hey, what are you doin' in there?" the night watchman called, and we heard some scurrying of feet.

Then somebody ran by us.

"Let's go!" said Gerald and we ran quietly up the matted steps and down the row towards the entrance. We ducked behind the last car near the entrance to see what was happening.

The night watchman and another man with little eyes and a big mouth had turned on some lights and were looking under the cars.

"I think she's over there," said the man with the big mouth.

Then to our left, on the other side of the row, we saw a girl dart out and run into Cobourg Street. I recognized her.

It was Fleurette Featherstone Fitchell!

She slipped on the greasy snow and fell down and we caught up to her. She was puffing and laughing and crying at the same time.

“Fleurette, what are you doing here?” I asked her once we were safe down the street.

“Nothing. Just playing,” Fleurette said, a really bold look in her eyes.

“Was there somebody else?” I said, thinking about the other running feet we had heard.

“Maybe,” Fleurette said, her chin stuck out.

“Who was it?” Gerald said.

“You won’t tell?” Fleurette said.

“No, we won’t tell,” I said. “Who was it?”

“It was Lester Lister,” she said. “Lester Lister. We were looking for something. Something he lost when we were here before once. He’s my boyfriend.”

She was very proud when she said that last thing. I knew Lester. He was in St. Albany’s choir with me. He didn’t come from around Angel Square. He came from Rockcliffe. He went to Ashdown School.

He was rich.

“What do you do here in dis awful place wid Lester Lister?” CoCo said, nudging me.

“Oh, things. Talk. Things.”

She was looking up into the falling Christmas snow. Then she said this:

“He lost his wallet. I was so scared. It was the night Sammy’s father got beat up.”

We were so surprised when she said this that we all started talking at once.

Suddenly she started to cry.

"I didn't see anything. I don't know anything." She was trying to rub the greasy snow off her legs where she fell down.

"You know someting," CoCo said. "What is it dat you know?"

"I don't know ANYTHING!" Fleurette screamed and ran down Cobourg Street into the night.

"It's none of your business!" she yelled out of the dark.

CoCo had to go home, so Gerald and I had to go over to Lester Lister's ourselves. If Fleurette wouldn't tell us anything, maybe Lester would.

I have to stop here a minute and tell you about Lester Lister and how I first met my best Dogan friend, Gerald Hickey.

Gerald moved in right near me on Cobourg Street last Christmas Day. That's when I met him.

Aunt Dottie had figured it would be a nice thing if I gave a guy named Lester Lister a present that Christmas Day because he was in the choir at St. Albany's and it was supposed to be nice to hang around with him because he was from Rockcliffe. I had to get on my good breeks and shine my rubber boots with floor wax and she helped me scrub my face until most of the skin was just about rubbed off.

Lester Lister was supposed to be a friend of mine.

Aunt Dottie said so.

We went over my own presents to see what one we

thought we should give to Lester Lister. It would have to be a good one because of where Lester lived. They had a big verandah and a cellar you didn't have to duck your head in. And they had a car and they had a phone and their radio could be turned right up so you could hear it.

And they had rugs on their floors.

Aunt Dottie decided I should give Lester Lister my best present but I knew I couldn't do that because my best present was the tank with the rubber tracks that would crawl over anything once you wound it up (even a pillow on the floor) and that tank was now crushed flat as a penny run over by a streetcar because my Uncle Paddy had stepped on it by mistake with one of his big army boots.

I guess it was all right that Uncle Paddy had done that to my tank because he didn't do it on purpose and besides, he was the one who bought it for me in the first place.

Aunt Dottie helped me wrap the present for Lester Lister.

We had chosen the flying propeller that you twirled down a long spiral rod to the bottom, then with a little gadget you pushed it up the rod, hard, and sent it spinning into the air. I hadn't given it a good workout because of the deep snow. Maybe next summer when Lester Lister got sick of it he'd give it back to me.

Aunt Dottie got out the ironing board and ironed some wrapping paper flat and then she got out a ruler and a razor blade and cut the paper into a perfect square. Then she made some paste out of flour and water and pasted up a perfect package. She cut out a piece of cardboard from a box into the shape of a bell and colored it with crayons.

Then she printed on the bell, "A special gift for my best friend, Lester. Merry Christmas."

"He's *not* my best friend," I said.

"Well, he's your *cleanest* friend," Aunt Dottie said, ignoring me.

"Why don't you put *that* then? 'To my cleanest friend, Lester'?"

"Don't be bold. It's Christmas," Aunt Dottie said. Then she put the package in a clean brown paper bag and folded the top of the bag over a few times so that it made a solid handle. Then she cut a hole in the handle for my four fingers to fit through.

I felt like Little Red Riding Hood or somebody being sent off to Granny's.

My Uncle Paddy and Dad were snoring in all the rooms. My sister Pamela was at her window.

I went out into the Christmas Day snow and from the sidewalk I gave Pamela a wave. The frost on the window was thick and made a beautiful pattern like fern leaves. In the middle of the fern leaves in the space where she had breathed away the frost, was Pamela's face.

It was like a holy painting.

I walked up Cobourg Street to the corner of

Papineau. I was trying to figure out what I would say when Mr. Lister or Mrs. Lister opened the door. I knew Lester Lister wouldn't open the door. He didn't seem the type. I guess he wasn't allowed. It was always one of his parents. Mostly Mr. Lister. I often wondered if sometime it would be Mr. Lister's sister who answered the door. But I didn't even know whether Mr. Lister had a sister. It would have made things interesting, though.

"Tommy, I'd like to have you meet Mr. Lister's sister Esther." And maybe if another long-lost aunt or somebody came in and they were all happy to see each other and kissing and stuff, somebody might say "Mr. Lister's sister kissed her, she sure has missed her!"

I was trying to figure out how to put in blister and pissed her pants when suddenly out jumped Gerald Hickey from behind a huge snowbank. I was right in front of Gerald Hickey's house. It was the worst house on the whole street. It was even worse than ours.

"Where'ya going?" Gerald said and he spit in the snow.

"What's it to you?" I said.

"Never mind then," said Gerald, who was very proud.

"To Lester Lister's in Rockcliffe," I said, just to see what he'd say.

"What for?" He spit and got some on my waxed rubber boot.

"I have to give him this Christmas present."

Gerald Hickey hocked one clean over the snowbank.

He was the best spitter around. The day was quiet with the few Christmas flakes coming down and no streetcars and only one dog way up around Heney Park probably barking.

Gerald Hickey and I were looking down Papineau Street towards Angel Square. I was wondering if we were going to have to fight. That was what you were supposed to do with new people who just moved in. Then, off the square and on up Papineau Street from the square, we saw two figures coming.

I knew they were Bodnoffs. Two tough Bodnoff brothers.

We waited and faced them as they got bigger and bigger coming up the empty silent Christmas street.

I hit the first Bodnoff across the side of the head with Lester Lister's present and knocked him down. Just when he hit the snowbank I scooped up a mittfull of snow and ground it into his face. I throttled him with his scarf for a while until I could see his eyes cross. I asked him politely if he wanted more and when he didn't I went to help Gerald with the other Bodnoff. We each took a leg and played wishbone with him until he asked us to stop. After a while we stopped and the two Bodnoffs went back down Papineau towards the square and got smaller and smaller. One of them was walking funny.

Gerald spit into the snowbanks and we went across the street to Provost's store and got one cent's worth of blackballs.

We opened the present the rest of the way and gave the propeller a few good spins.

Then Gerald sent it up so high over the low small roofs of Lowertown that it got lost against the gray Christmas clouds and if it came down at all we didn't see it and we didn't hear it.

Then Gerald Hickey and I went to Gerald Hickey's house and practiced wrestling in Gerald Hickey's coalbin for about an hour.

Then I went home to try and explain to Aunt Dottie.

That was almost a year before.

Now we were going to Rockcliffe for real. A real reason.

To solve a crime.

It was snowing tons of snow. Snow floating down in beautiful tons.

We walked over the St. Patrick Street Bridge and up Springfield Road on to Acacia Drive and into Rockcliffe Village where everybody was rich.

All the streets in Rockcliffe are called Avenue and Way and Terrace and View and Place and Drive and Vista and names like that.

In Lowertown all the streets are called Street. Cobourg Street. Friel Street. Augusta Street. York Street. If a street was really in bad shape (houses all falling over and broken sheds and fences full of holes and broken windows and raggedy kids and older brothers back from the war always drunk) it wouldn't even be called a street.

Like Papineau, for instance. Not Papineau Street, just Papineau. You ask Chalmers Lonnigan, "Where do you live, Chalmers?"

"I live on Papineau."

"Is that a street or an avenue?"

"I dunno."

Gerald and I had been together in Rockcliffe before.

We specially liked to go over right after supper when it was dark. We'd have our supper about five-thirty or six but the people in Rockcliffe had their supper about half past seven or eight. Rich people eat later for some reason.

Maybe it was because they weren't very hungry.

Lester Lister told me it wasn't called supper anyway. It was called dinner.

In Lowertown we ate our dinner at noon.

In Rockcliffe they'd have their dinner at suppertime and their lunch at dinner time.

Pretty confusing.

We'd gone over a couple of times when there wasn't much to do and looked in people's windows. We weren't looking in windows in Rockcliffe to see people taking their clothes off or anything like that. We'd look to see what they were having for supper (dinner) and try to guess what they were saying to each other by reading their lips.

It was hard to figure out what they were saying. Whatever it was, it didn't look very interesting. They weren't talking about germs, that's for sure, or turkeys.

Sometimes they wouldn't say anything for a long time. They'd just look at their fireplaces or their plates and not move their lips at all.

They were probably thinking about important matters concerning the world or Germans or something.

Or maybe they were all just thinking about money.

We arrived at Lester's fancy house and went up on the big verandah and rang the bell.

Gerald spit over the railing just as Mrs. Lister opened the door.

"Could I speak to Lester for a moment, please?" I said.

Mrs. Lister looked at Gerald and me like we were some kind of Martians or something.

"I'm afraid he's having dinner at the moment," she said. (It was about nine o'clock at night so of course they were having dinner.)

"It's about school," I said. "It's really very important."

"Just a moment then," she said, and left us standing out there in the cold.

Pretty soon Lester came out, slipping on a fur hat so he wouldn't get his brain exposed to the winter. As soon as he closed the door and stepped out on the verandah, Gerald crowded him up against the wall.

"Tonight you were in the car barns doing naughty things with Miss Fleurette Featherstone Fitchell and looking for your wallet which you lost the night somebody beat up Sammy Rosenberg's father. You and Miss Fitchell saw something that night that she won't tell us about but that you *will* tell us about because if you don't, we're going to spoil your dinner by telling Mummy and Daddy that you are studying hamburger buns and cigars with Miss Fitchell some nights instead of being where you're supposed to be, wherever that is."

It was so easy. For Gerald.

Yes, they were there, Lester said, in a whiny voice, they were there, but he's never going there again, honest, and that night they heard the yelling and they saw the man in the hood and they saw him hit Mr. Rosenberg and they saw him run away after Mr. Rosenberg fell down and they saw something fall out of the man's pocket and they were so scared but Fleurette picked it up and they ran out and when they reached the entrance a man stopped them and said that they'd better not say anything to anyone about this or they'd be awful sorry and then they ran home.

"What did she pick up, Lester? What was it?" I said.

"It was just a comic," said Lester. "Just a stupid comic book. It fell out of the man's pocket." Lester was fiddling with his fur hat.

"Okay, Lester," Gerald said, "go in and finish your dinner." Lester went in and shut the door quietly.

We stood on the St. Patrick Street Bridge for a while watching the ice and talking and then we went home.

cards. I made a card for him with a picture of a moon eclipse on it and some little noiseless bells.

I wrote this on it:

Merry Christmas, Mr. Maynard. I loved what you said about the leaf on the moon.
Tommy

Then the bell rang and everybody ran out on Angel Square and tried to get home. The school was suddenly quiet.

I slipped into Blue Cheeks's room and wrote a Christmas message on his empty blackboard. It was a sentence he could have a lot of Christmas fun correcting over the holidays.

It said this:

The boy wrote Merry Christmas to his teacher and then quietly left the room on the blackboard.
Signed
The Shadow

It was his favorite kind of sentence. A wrong one.

I met "Fitchy" in the schoolyard and walked with her to her house on Friel Street.

"I don't like Lester Lister anymore, anyway," she said. "He ran away and left me. He's a coward."

I waited outside her back door while she went in to get the comic. There were a whole lot of cats under her

A comic book.
Just a comic book.
But it was something.
It was a clue.

4 L

BY FRIDAY there was so much snow that every plough was out and the teams of men and the big sleighs were out all day and all night.

Each box sleigh is pulled by a team of horses and each sleigh has one driver and ten shovelers. The horses stand in a cloud of their own steam and their whiskers are frozen white and their manes hang down with gobs of ice. The ten shovelers shovel the snowbank into the sleigh and shout and swear and laugh and sing and play jokes on each other.

And that day the bells on all the harnesses were tinkling and jingling in Lowertown on the last day of school before Christmas, the first Christmas after the war.

Angel Square was raging; everybody was trying to get a good day of fighting in before the holiday.

All over the square the Jews and the Dogans and the

Pea Soups were running headfirst into eac
mountain goats.

At school Blue Cheeks was in a very C
mood and only gave out lines to Killer Bo
Fleurette Featherstone Fitchell for passing p
hamburger buns and cigars back and forth.

I wrote a note to Fleurette and passed it to
Blue Cheeks wasn't looking.

FFF.
Lester said you have the comic book the
dropped in the car barns that night.
I want it.
If you don't give it to me I'll tell Mrs. Lister a
you and Lester and you'll never see him again
Signed
Tommy

I watched her face as she read it. She was movi
lips.

When she was finished she looked over at m
nodded.

Her note to me said this:

Meet me after school gets out.
Signed
Fitchy

We were getting out at noon and so our last class
with Mr. Maynard. We sat around chatting and maki

back shed looking out at me standing there in the falling snow.

She came back out with the comic but she didn't give it to me right away.

"Do you want to come in the back shed with me?"

"I can't," I lied. "I've got to go to work."

"He was going to give me a watch for Christmas," she said.

"It's better this way," I said and I touched the hand that was holding the comic.

"I guess so," she said. "Lester Lister is a coward." She let go of the comic.

"You're not a coward, though," she said.

"Thank you," I said.

"It's okay if you call me Fitchy."

"Thank you, Fitchy."

On the way home I studied the comic book. It was a war comic with different pictures of Japs and Germans being stabbed and blown up.

Up on the corner somebody had written an initial.

The letter L.

The man who hit Sammy's father had written that letter there maybe.

L.

At home, while my sister Pamela was crushing me at the door, I could smell cake and fruit. Usually I didn't smell anything at our house. Funny how other people's houses smell like something but your own never does. Maybe it's because you're so used to your own house.

Gerald Hickey's house always smelled like onions and starch.

Sammy's house always smelled like incense and pickles and fish.

CoCo Laframboise's house smelled like beans and pie.

Lester Lister's house smelled like shellac.

Dad was home early too and he and Aunt Dottie were talking about turkeys and chickens again and this time Dad was saying he was having trouble getting *chickens* even and how Devine's and the other stores in the market were all out of them.

They were saying that it looked like we were going to have to have Mock Duck again.

Mock Duck is a big slab of meat piled up with dressing and then rolled up like a jelly roll and tied up with lots of thick string.

One Christmas my Uncle Paddy ate a piece of string from the Mock Duck about as long as his arm and Dad and I went out in the kitchen with him to help him pull it all out. It reminded me of a movie I once saw where Laurel and Hardy ate some wool socks and had to pull the long threads out of their mouths at a fancy dinner.

Aunt Dottie said Uncle Paddy ruined our whole dinner. I guess she was right. It wasn't very Christmassy watching a guy eat string for about fifteen minutes.

But I like my Uncle Paddy. He's a nice man. He's pretty cuddly. And big. Even bigger than Dad. He's in the Air Force Police. He is a very loud sneezer. Once he sneezed so loud that the cat ran headfirst into a wall.

Uncle Paddy has huge arms and wrists. One of his wrists is thicker than Gerald Hickey's neck. So is the other one.

Dad was putting on his coat and his scarf and was saying he had to go up to the Union Station to meet the soldiers coming in. One of his friends would be there. He was a Cameron Highlander.

His name was Frank. Back from the war.

I said I'd go with him because I had to go uptown to some stores to hunt for some Christmas presents.

We got off the streetcar and walked across Rideau Street into the Union Station. The *U* in the word *Union* was shaped like a *V*.

We went over to talk to a Red Cap in a red cap, a cousin of Dad's from up the Gatineau who stuttered. They talked and laughed for a few minutes and we talked about money then the Red Cap reached in his pouch where all his tips were and filled my hand with nickles.

"Merry Chri-Chri-Chri-Chri..." he said. "Come back to-to-to-tomorrow and I'll give you some more."

There were mobs of people all bundled up and stamping snow and we started down the long wide stairs to where all the thousands of soldiers were with their knapsacks and gear. Everybody was kissing and hugging and running and squealing and crying. Over the loud-speakers, Bing Crosby was singing "I'm Dreaming of a White Christmas." There was a huge Christmas tree twinkling in the middle of the floor and decorations and streamers crawled up the walls.

You had to lean way back to see the ceiling.

Steam floated in through the iron gates where the trains were.

We waited and watched for about a half an hour but there was no sign of Dad's friend Frank. Dad met one soldier he knew who said yes, Frank was on the train but he didn't know where he was now.

Dad said he'd go down to the market and look for him around there, so I said goodbye and went hunting for presents.

I went to Charles Ogilvy's, Murphy Gamble's, Bryson Graham's, Reitman's, Caplan's, Lindsay's, Orme's, Shaf-fer's, Stein's, Larocque's and Freiman's.

It was in Freiman's I saw it.

It was on the glass counter with a sign beside it. The sign said "For that girl of girls." Then there was a picture of Rita Hayworth.

Richard Hudnut's Three Flower Gift Set

Picture her rapture on finding this set
beneath the tree Christmas morn.
Soft green embossed gift box contains
Hudnut's lovely

FACE POWDER, ROUGE, LIPSTICK,
TOILET WATER, PERFUME, TALCUM,
VANISHING CREAM, BRILLIANTINE,
COLOGNE AND CLEANSING CREAM.

$7.50

I put two dollars down and asked the lady if she could hold the Richard Hudnut Three Flower Gift Set until Monday, the day before Christmas. Then I would bring in the rest of the money.

She said that I could.

She had a face like she was a sort of Virgin Mary. A little bit of a little smile, eyes looking up and to the right, head a bit on one side, and a halo sitting just over her head with nothing holding it up.

But it wasn't really a halo, it was some silver spray on a mirror right behind her.

In Freiman's I also found a duck for my sister Pamela. I always got her a little yellow duck made of rubber. You squeezed the duck and it went quack for you.

She really enjoyed the duck even though she got the same thing the year before. It was always like a new present because she didn't have very much of a memory. Every day she'd have to find out about squeezing the duck and making it do a quack. And she'd always laugh just like it never happened before. Every day she had a chance to be happy. Then the duck would be worn out by summer and Aunt Dottie would throw it away and she'd forget all about it.

Then the next Christmas, the duck, all over again, and happy, all over again.

She was lucky in a way, not knowing anything. She didn't have to know about Sammy's dad or a man named L or anything about the war or the fights on Angel Square or the Ritchie's Feed and Seed bags or Delbert Dilabio or Arnie Sultzburger.

Maybe she was lucky.

Or maybe not.

She also didn't know about Gerald or Sammy or CoCo or the lovely Margot Lane or Lamont Cranston or The Shadow or Mr. Maynard.

Maybe she wasn't lucky.

I don't know.

Then, in Freiman's, I saw Dad's present.

It was a Flat Fifty.

A Flat Fifty is a tin box (flat) with fifty cigarettes inside. You buy them for special occasions or if you have fancy tables in your house you can put one of these fancy flat tins out so that your guests can help themselves, don't mind if I do.

I buy Dad a Flat Fifty every Christmas. I always mean to change and get him something different but for some reason, just at the last minute, I wind up getting him another Flat Fifty. It's almost like being hypnotized. I'd be determined not to get him a Flat Fifty again but then I'd be in a store, Christmas shopping, and I'd see all the Flat Fifties stacked up with Christmas bows on them and I'd go over, pulled over there by some big magnet, and my mouth would open and I'd hear it say, "Flat Fifty, please."

I couldn't seem to help it.

And Christmas morning Dad would pick up his present from me and he'd weigh it in his hands and he'd feel the shape of it and he'd say, "I hope it's a Flat Fifty!" and then he'd rip the paper off.

"It is! It is a Flat Fifty! Just what I wanted. Thank you very much!" he would always say. And then when Aunt Dottie was opening hers from me (I always got her chocolates, I couldn't help it) Dad would say, "I wonder if it's chocolates." And then when Aunt Dottie would finally get it open (it took her about an hour to unwrap because she wouldn't tear the paper) Dad would yell, "It is! It is chocolates! Let's have a couple!"

"No, you're not having any, I'm saving these for *myself* for a change this year," Aunt Dottie would say and put them on the floor beside her.

(Uncle Paddy was there one Christmas Day and stepped in Aunt Dottie's chocolates by mistake—squashed every one of them.)

Then, after we helped Pamela open her duck and got her to squeeze it and make it quack a few times, Aunt Dottie would send me down the cellar to the cold storage to bring up some shortbread with the half cherry on each one and the Christmas cake wrapped in wax paper and we'd have a little snack.

So I went over to the counter with the Flat Fifties all stacked up with the Christmas bows on them and my mouth opened and I heard it say, "Flat Fifty, please!"

That was enough shopping.

I walked home through the gently falling snow. The lights from the people's windows along York Street were yellow and warm. Some cats picked their way into the laneways.

I passed the school and crossed Angel Square all alone. It was a beautiful square in the late winter afternoon.

All alone on Angel Square.

I came up Papineau and turned the corner onto Cobourg Street.

Dad and some soldiers were out in front of our house taking pictures of each other. One soldier, who seemed to be quite clumsy and off balance all the time, was trying to take a picture of Dad and the other two soldiers. Dad was in the middle. He had one arm around each soldier.

The soldier taking the picture was looking down into the camera, shading it with one hand and backing up, trying to get everybody in the picture. He had the camera down about at his waist and he had one eye closed while he backed up the side of the snowbank.

Quite a few people saw him when he fell backwards over the bank and did a complete backroll and got his head stuck in the deep snow. The camera flew out onto the streetcar tracks.

A streetcar with a driver and two inspectors was going slowly by, heading for the car barn; a lot of kids, making their snow forts, stopped and watched; three people pushing a car onto Desjardins Street saw; Chalmers Lonnigan peeking around Papineau saw; some Dogans looking out over their half-built snow fort up from St. Patrick Street saw; Aunt Dottie upstairs in her poem room, probably looking out, saw; Pamela, for sure, looking out her window through her frost frame saw.

It was Dad's friend Frank home from the war.

The streetcar quietly crushed the camera.

I took the comic over to Gerald's house and we studied it. We took it over to CoCo's house and we studied it.

L.

That night I went to my choir practice at St. Albany's Anglican Church.

I went up the hill on King Edward to the corner of Daly and followed in the deep footprints around the side of the church where some of the others in the choir had stepped. I went through the little green door and down the wooden stairs to the practice room.

It's a room like the room at Talmud Torah where I do the floors. There are even pictures on the walls caps; they have on black cassocks and white surplices.

Lester Lister was standing beside me, singing. In the middle of the hymn we had a conversation. It was easy. You sang what you wanted to say instead of the words in the Hymn Book.

Instead of:

Holy, Holy, Holy,
Merciful and Mighty
God in three persons
Blessed Trinity

I sang:

Got the comic from her
Says she doesn't like you
Says you are a coward
'cause you ran away.

When the hymn got to the second finish, instead of the real words, Lester sang:

I don't like her either
She's just a dirty slut
Now I can forget about
The watch I said I'd buy.

Lester Lister. What a slimy person.

I knew Gerald would meet me after practice because he always did on Fridays.

I walked slowly up Rideau Street waiting for him to surprise me like he always did. It was a game we played. If he got me, I would buy the drinks; if I saw him first, he would buy.

He was nowhere in sight.

Then I felt the gun in my back. I was about halfway home coming up Rideau Street on the north side right near Imbro's Restaurant.

Usually I would turn into Imbro's (and Gerald and I would have a cream soda), his gun still on me the whole time.

"Turn in here, copper," Gerald would say, "and don't look around or I'll drill ya!"

Inside the restaurant I'd have my hands up, not high but halfway up and wrists a little loose. Gerald would push me over into a booth for two near the door.

"Two cream sodas, doll, and be quick about it!" Gerald would say to the waitress. She would smile and be right back with the two bottles. I would pay the fourteen cents.

"Okay, sucker," Gerald would say, "drink up and let's scram, pigeon!"

Then, if the waitress came by again, Gerald might say: "You know, honey, you're much prettier when you're angry!"

The girl would just laugh because she was used to

this. She'd heard it all before. It was the same every Friday night. Every time I got paid at choir.

"Stop that eternal pacing up and down!" Gerald might say to Louis, the owner, if he was around.

"A man like you could have an accident on the street, for instance. Hit and run driver maybe. You never know." They were things that people said in movies. Gerald would have his hat pulled down over his eyes and a fake cigarette hanging out of the corner of his mouth.

Louis would just laugh. He'd heard it all before. On Friday nights. My pay night at choir.

Outside, the Friday night was dressed up for Christmas on Rideau Street. The hydro poles were wrapped in boughs and the streetcars had a wreath in each front window. The shops had Coca Cola Santas hung up in the windows and some had small Christmas trees with flashing lights. Imbro's had some bells on the door and if you went out into the middle of Rideau Street and looked downtown, you could see a big tree on top of Freiman's and maybe a lot of other blue and red colors down there.

Gerald and I did part of our game with the waitress and Louis and then we discussed the comic.

Gerald said he thought that the L could stand for Lonnigan. Chalmers Lonnigan's father. He hated Jews. It might be him. It was worth a try. Gerald said he thought he worked at the museum.

I said goodbye to Gerald and went home.

Dad and I listened to part of the Friday night fights on the radio.

It was Tony Janero and Humberto Zavala. We didn't find out who won because the tubes got weak in the middle of round seven.

Finally all we could hear was the cat purring and now and then a streetcar going home to the barns, the rumbling muffled by the snow, shaking the house a little bit.

Aunt Dottie had hung some balsam boughs on the wall going upstairs. They smelled deep and fresh.

I went to sleep with Christmas in my nose and Margot Lane in my head.

Tomorrow Gerald and CoCo and I would have a talk with Chalmers Lonnigan and see if we could find out anything.

5 Something Ice Cold

SATURDAY MORNING I was sitting with my sister Pamela at her window trying to show her how to make shapes on the glass in the frost with her hands.

I made a moon shape and a sun and some stars but they weren't very good and she didn't understand. She wouldn't have understood anyway, even if I had made them better. She was having fun though, mostly because of how the frost made her fingers cold.

I made a shape of a duck on another part of the window just to see if she'd remember. She looked at it for a long time and pointed at it once and looked at me but then she forgot about it and started to hug me a little bit.

I think she was trying to remember but she couldn't.

Through the duck I could see Chalmers Lonnigan standing out there. He was standing on the snowbank, way up, his face up to the sky, his tongue out, catching snowflakes.

Since I didn't have enough money yet to finish my Christmas shopping and I had nothing to do until Gerald came over, I went out to have a little talk with him.

"Thinking about heaven, Chalmers?" I said.

"Do you want to go and hurt some Jews?" Chalmers said.

"No, I don't. No, I don't want to go and hurt some Jews, Chalmers," I said.

"Why not?" Chalmers said.

"Because," I said. "Why don't you go uptown or something or go to the show or read some comics or something?"

"I don't want to," Chalmers said.

"Well, I don't want to either," I said.

"Why don't you want to?" Chalmers said.

"Because my best friend Sammy is a Jew and he lends me his cap gun whenever I want and I lend him my cap gun every time he wants and I even sort of like his cousin Shirley from Toronto. I tried to kiss her once."

The last part was a lie but you had to tell Chalmers *something* to try and make him understand.

"Okay," Chalmers said, "let's go and get some Pea Soups then. There's some behind Brébeuf playing tunnel right now, I think."

"I don't feel like it," I said. Then I changed the subject.

I said: "How's your father?"

"Let's get some Protestants then," he said. Chalmers was really looking hard for something to do. I tried again.

"They're not easy to find," I said. "I don't even think there *are* any Protestants around here anymore." Poor Chalmers. How was he going to get to heaven this way? "Is it true your father works at the museum?"

He left a big silence. Then he started talking again.

"There used to be lots of them all over the place. My father told me that they used to kill them with streetcars." He had a sound in his voice like somebody was talking about their favorite cat that got lost or their brother who was kidnapped or something.

"There was only one or two," I said, "and I think they moved away."

"Where did they move to?"

"Uptown somewhere."

"There's lots of Dogans. Let's go get a few Dogans."

"Chalmers! *You're* a Dogan. And anyway, it's Christmas! You're supposed to be nice to people on Christmas!"

"Why?"

"Because Jesus said."

"No he didn't."

"Jesus was a Jew, you know," I said right to his eyes.

A look came on Chalmer's face like a streetcar had just run over his foot.

Just then Gerald Hickey popped up from behind the

snowbank. I guess he had heard everything we said because he winked at me and started talking like on "The Green Hornet," a radio program we listened to.

Just to tease Chalmers.

"Word is out they found a Protestant down on Augusta Street. A bunch of Dogans is going over to interrogate him. Bodnoff and the Bodnoffs are getting a gang of their Jews together to invent some tortures for him and the Pea Soups are over there right now breaking down his snow fort. Want to go and watch?"

Chalmers was already running. He couldn't wait.

We met CoCo on the corner and went over to where the Protestant was supposed to be on Augusta Street but there was nobody there.

"Maybe it's a trap," Gerald said.

"Let's wait in the laneway for a while and see who shows up," Chalmers said.

Somebody had shoveled a path through the deep snow in the laneway and we started down the path but then we stopped. There was a big gang of Pea Soups in there arguing and fighting. They had one Pea Soup headfirst in a snow hole and they were shoving him farther down. We turned back.

We went two laneways down. There, the Bodnoffs and their Jews were plotting. They were discussing a snowman they had surrounded. It had a whole lot of sticks stuck in it and a sign around its neck. The sign said, Dogan or Pea Soup.

Behind the next garage a whole lot of Dogans were fighting each other, ripping each others' clothes.

There wasn't much to do on the Christmas holidays.

"I guess they're practising for when school goes back," Gerald said.

"Where's the Protestant?" said Chalmers, almost crying.

Then he turned around to go home.

Before he left he made a little speech.

"I'm going home. There's nothing to do. I wish I was dead and in heaven," he said. Then he left.

"Let's cut across Angel Square and go uptown," CoCo said. "What did he tell you? Anyting?"

"Nothing," I said.

We walked across Angel Square. It was very peaceful and white. There were no people fighting on the square because school was out. There weren't even any footprints in the perfect snow.

We walked up York Street right into the market and past Devine's and Ritchie's Feed and Seed and R. Hector Aubrey's meat store.

I saw Blue Cheeks coming out of Aubrey's with a bag of meat. He saw me but I got my eyes away just in time. I didn't want to spoil Christmas.

I saw CoCo Laframboise's uncle, Toe-Jam Laframboise, getting into his delivery truck. His boots were covered with snow and he was knocking them on the side of his truck. I knew that underneath his boots his socks were stuck to his feet forever.

We went up to the Chateau Laurier and slipped in the front door past the doorman and ran up the curving ruggy stairs with the gold polished railings all the way to the top floor.

We played Abbot and Costello on each floor with the fancy furniture on the landings. We pretended we were eating the furniture and that we were in a hypnotic trance that made us think we were termites. It was from a movie we saw once.

We slid all the way down the railings past the lobby and down into the floor where the swimming pool was and the entrance to the tunnel. The doors of the tunnel were hard to open because of the suction. We walked down the tunnel under Rideau Street like robots from a movie we saw once. We were coming from a lost underground city.

At the other end of the tunnel, in the Union Station, in the men's toilet, we twisted all the handles on the pay toilets like it was a big time machine. But it wasn't the same without Sammy.

I saw the Red Cap and he told me if I came back later he might have some more extra change for me.

We left the Union Station and headed for the museum. But first we sneaked through the Fire Escape door of the Capitol Theatre on Bank Street. The kids were starting to line up outside for the holiday show. It was

"Captain Kidd," starring Charles Laughton. But we weren't going to stay.

We were upstairs above the main lobby. The red plush curtains were all around us. The theater was still closed. It was like a palace for a Pharaoh.

There was marble and brass and copper shining all around us.

And big, curving stairs with marble railings curving up and the smell of popcorn and chocolate and the sound of feet on quiet rugs. I could see the box office down there and could remember the feel of the tickets—your little ticket in your hand that smelled like sweet cardboard when you were a little kid.

And the uniforms of the ushers like little soldiers. And their hats. And their white gloves, turned down. And their shiny black shoes and the exit signs in red and black and the paintings on the wall as you went down the wide winding stairs.

And the smell of dust and popcorn and darkness and the sound of the travelogue music maybe playing up the wide stairs, when you were a kid at your first show.

All this was making me sad.

All these things reminded me of Sammy.

It was time to go to the museum but instead we ran up to the Supreme Court and stood on the wide steps and played capital punishment. Gerald pronounced sentence on me:

"You will be taken from this place to another place

where you will be hanged by the neck until you are dead and may God have mercy on your soul!" said Gerald in a sad, serious voice.

I bowed my head.

It was from many movies we once saw.

It was time to go to the museum. But we didn't. Scared maybe. Instead we went down Bank Street and we went into the U-Wanta Lunch restaurant and had some chips and gravy and the cook threw on some cranberries because it was Christmas and Gerald let the cranberries run out the side of his mouth and pretended he was shot until the waitress got worried and CoCo laughed and we left and went down Argyle Street to the museum and went through the heavy doors. Here at last. Suddenly the huge silence was on us.

Looking for Mr. Lonnigan.

Inside it smelled like rug dust, preserves, dried rose leaves inside a Bible. There were oak railings and brass knobs and marble stairs, marble walls and glass cases. I felt the buffalo's glass eyes. You feel them with your thumb and fingers when the Commissionaire isn't looking.

The silence was humming quietly and then a little kid's voice went all the way to the ceiling from somewhere with the sound of the paintings just hanging there and the sound of dinosaurs standing there, just in their bones; maybe the sound of bubbling water, soft, in the fish tanks; maybe a quiet Commissionaire in his dark blue uniform talking loudly because he was sort of old and a bit deaf maybe.

And we played movie around the elevator cables and cement gargoyles and long staircases, doors covered with padding, people holding hands, a scarf lying in a big marble room, faces looking through railings. Three floors up in a big glass room an Eskimo stood beside his hole in the ice beside his dead fish with blood on it. We stood still there and watched him for a while. We stood the way he was standing, waiting to see if he'd move before we did. But he didn't. He was never going to move. Sammy and I had often been here.

And on the art gallery floor I saw a guy looking at a huge painting that was covered in glass. He was right up close to the painting and I thought he must really know a lot about paintings to be standing that close.

But then he wiped his hand over his hair and I realized he was looking at his own reflection in the glass. He wasn't looking at the painting at all. He was checking his hair.

We asked the Commissionaire if he knew Mr. Lonnigan.

Sure he did, but Mr. Lonnigan didn't work there any more. Not for more than six months now.

"In fact," the Commissionaire said, "I heard he left town and went to the States. Left his family and just took off. Not a very nice man. Not a very nice thing to do."

So that was why Chalmers wouldn't talk about him.

Poor Chalmers.

Then we went to the Français Theatre on Dalhousie Street to see the two o'clock show. It was twelve cents to get in.

We saw the guys ride horses. Ride up to an old mine site up in the rocks somewhere. There was a car parked outside a cabin. A car and some horses.

We saw the hero. He had a square face and his pants were high. He had a shirt on and his tie was undone.

He was fighting in some underground mine tunnel with three other guys who didn't have ties on and who were very ugly.

The fight lasted about half the show. They rolled around in the dirt and the music was loud and exciting.

A girl was standing with her back pressed against the wall of the tunnel, one hand in her mouth.

A gunpowder keg got knocked over and rolled along, leaving a trail which became a fuse when the girl knocked a flaming torch from the wall as she tried to help out the guy in the high pants. Girls were so useless. They were nice, though. You hated to see them get mutilated or shot or thrown in hot tubs of boiling lava or eaten by about forty crocodiles or blown up in some mine.

It wasn't a very good show, so I decided to leave.

I told Gerald and CoCo about my Richard Hudnut present for Margot Lane and how I'd be getting it Monday when the rest of my money came in. Then I left.

Money. Outside in the falling snow I decided to drop

by the Union Station again to see if Red Cap meant it when he said for me to come back and he'd give me some more change. Every cent counted.

I found him at his usual spot and we talked about Christmas and money. I told him about all my jobs and he said that it was very good to have all those jobs.

Then he suggested another way of making money. He said he liked reading comics and if I had any that he hadn't read he'd buy them from me. Then he said that he knew other people who would buy them from me too. It would be a very good business to be in. In fact, some of the people who would buy them lived right near me on Cobourg Street.

One man specially.

He would buy all the comics I had.

Specially the war comics.

The violent ones.

"He lives right on your street. Works in the car b-b-b-barns there. Mechanic. Loves to read c-c-c-comics!"

The station was crowded and busy. All the Christmas travelers were going somewhere or coming from somewhere. There was Christmas music coming over the loud-speakers.

I could feel the back of my neck bristling.

I could feel gooseflesh on my arms.

I felt like I was standing near something very evil.

I felt terror.

I heard myself ask the question.

"What's this man's name?"

"L-L-L-L-Logg. M-M-M-Mister Logg."

All of a sudden the whole Union Station seemed to stop. Everything around me was like a picture. I walked up the wide stairs through the frozen crowds and the dead silence hearing only my own heart pounding in my ears.

L for Logg.

I went to Sammy's to see if there was anybody there. The apartment hall was dark and sad and nobody answered the door.

I went to the car barns and asked one of the drivers if he knew Mr. Logg.

"Sure, that's him over there," he said, pointing to a big man with his back to us, washing his hands in a sink.

I walked over to him as he was drying his hands. I stood behind him. I could smell evil.

"Mr. Logg?" I said.

He turned around.

He had little eyes and a big mouth.

Something ice cold ran up my back.

He looked down at me without saying a word.

"Would you like to buy some comics?"

"Maybe. Got any?"

"Yes."

"Bring them over to my place."

"Where do you live?"

"Thirty-two Cobourg Street, Apartment 406," he said, his little eyes burning.

At home Aunt Dottie was glaring at Dad's friend Frank. He had walked in with his army boots and tracked snow all over the place. They were talking about the Mock Duck and how there were definitely no turkeys or chickens because of the war that was over.

Frank was standing there picking his nose a little bit and Dad was asking him if he liked Mock Duck and would he like to come over on Christmas and have dinner with us.

Supper with us. Sipper with us.

Then Frank tried to go into the kitchen to get some water for his drink but he stepped on the cat and fell down before he got to the sink.

Then Dad asked him if maybe he'd like to come over Christmas Eve too and enjoy the tree since he was a bachelor and had no family to spend Christmas with.

My sister Pamela gave him a big hug after he got up and then he started to sing some army song and Aunt Dottie just kept glaring at him.

After supper (Aunt Dottie wouldn't pass him the butter when he asked for it and when he reached over to get it he spilled the jug of milk) I called on Gerald and we went over to CoCo's and had a meeting.

They were so excited they could hardly talk.

"It must be him," Gerald said. "We've got him! We've got him!"

"You're going over dere," CoCo said. "You must be very very careful, *tabarnac*!"

We went out into Lowertown and went to everybody's house we knew.

After a couple of hours we had collected almost fifty comics.

Many of them were just what Mr. Logg would enjoy.

6 Beyond a Shadow of a Doubt

EARLY SUNDAY MORNING I got up and made myself some Quaker. I looked at him and he looked at me as I ate. He looked pretty wise. He followed me around the kitchen.

Maybe he knew about Mr. Logg.

Aunt Dottie had left me a message to deliver before I went to church to do my six A.M. altar boy job. She left two Christmas cards to deliver next door to the McIntoshes' house. I would put them in their mailbox early. That way the McIntoshes wouldn't see me.

It would save paying for the stamps.

There were two cards. One for Mrs. McIntosh and one for Mr. McIntosh. There were two cards because Mr. and Mrs. McIntosh didn't like each other and never spoke to each other.

Mr. McIntosh had wired up the fence around his yard

to keep the kids from climbing on it all the time. He had a switch in his cellar. He would wait until all the kids were on his fence and then he'd pull the switch and try to electrocute them all.

They'd all be screaming and diving off the fence and he'd be in his basement looking out the window with his hand on the switch and laughing. Mrs. McIntosh didn't like this. Whenever he did it, she would go into her cupboard and get out a whole lot of the homemade chocolates that she made all the time and go out and give them to all the kids.

Mr. McIntosh didn't like this.

While Mrs. McIntosh was handing out the chocolates, Mr. McIntosh would be in the cellar yelling and shaking his fist. You couldn't hear him yelling but you could see him.

That's why they never spoke to each other.

That's why Aunt Dottie sent over separate Christmas cards.

I put the cards quietly into the McIntoshes' mailbox and walked up St. Patrick Street to St. Brigit's Church through the dark and softly falling snow.

At ten to six I was in the sacristy with my surplice on, getting Father Foley ready for early mass.

It was interesting getting him ready for his show. He was a kind and gentle man with a nice face. Before I helped him get dressed up, he looked like any kind man you might see in a store or on the street or shoveling snow. But once he had his outfit on he became very special. He could have been in a movie.

While Father Foley was putting on his amice, I got his alb all smoothed out and ready. Then I put the alb on him, right sleeve first. Then I held the cincture for him, making sure the tassels were at my right. Then I gave him his maniple and he kissed it and hung it on his left arm. Then I gave him his long narrow stole for around his shoulders.

Finally I helped him on with his chasuble with all the gold and silver stitching.

He looked pretty nice. Pretty special.

Then we left the sacristy and went to the altar. I bowed a few times and went over to the credence table and fixed up the cruets of wine and water and the little wafers of bread.

There was a big crowd in church, everybody with their coats on, some coughing, a couple of babies crying a little bit. After "Alleluia" Father Foley read to us about what Jesus said on the hill.

I looked up at Jesus.

Jesus was up on his cross, blood on his forehead, in drops, dropping from his hands and his feet, some on his knees, and quite a bit coming out of his side.

Father Foley read: "How happy are the poor, happy the gentle; happy those who mourn; happy those who hunger; happy those who thirst for what is right; happy the merciful; happy the pure…happy…happy…happy."

It was a nice reading.

Later I went and got the wine cruet and the water cruet from the credence table. With my right hand I gave Father Foley the wine cruet after I kissed it. Then I gave him the water cruet with my right hand after I kissed it and got the wine cruet back in my left hand and kissed it again.

Then I got the plate and the towel and I helped Father Foley wash his hands.

Later, when Father Foley lifted up the chalice, with my right hand I rang the bell and with my thumb and finger of my left hand I held up his beautiful chasuble.

And I tried to whisper the mystery with Father Foley but I couldn't.

Then the people were lining up and kneeling along the rail and I was following Father Foley with the silver tray and the cloth, holding it under each chin of each person as each one took his bread and his wine.

The next chin raised up and a big furry tongue came out and over that the eyes opened and met my eyes.

I thought I heard somebody stab an organ somewhere.

Mr. Logg!

Mr. Logg in church with all these nice people.

And only two or three of us in church knew about what Mr. Logg had done.

Mr. Logg knew.

I knew.

And Jesus probably knew.

Then I got my idea.

More than the three of us should know about Mr. Logg and what he did. Many, many more.

After mass I got my pay (four dollars for eight Sundays) and I went home.

One shopping day until Christmas.

Tomorrow.

When I got home it was getting light and my sister Pamela was at her window and gave me a big welcome when I came in.

Aunt Dottie was up scrubbing and waxing everything for Christmas and Dad went out and got the *Star Weekly*, the Sunday paper.

I loved the smell of the *Star Weekly* and the cold feel of it when he brought it in. I smelled the ink of the funnies and lay down on the floor and read them.

They were all doing Christmas things in the funnies. Blondie and Popeye and Invisible Scarlet O'Neil and Dick Tracy and Andy Gump and Little Orphan Annie were all talking about Christmas.

Even Superman and Tarzan and Red Ryder were doing Christmas things.

The only one in the funnies who wasn't doing Christmas things was Alley Oop. Alley Oop was a caveman and didn't know anything about Christmas because Christmas wasn't invented yet in caveman days.

I helped Aunt Dottie wax the floor. I shook some ashes and I helped Dad put up the tree.

My sister Pamela was so excited that she started to howl and cry. We calmed her down with some shortbread that Aunt Dottie was just taking out of the oven.

I untangled the Christmas tree lights for Aunt Dottie and laid them out in a long string on the floor for her and then went to my room to sit on the bed and think.

It was time.

I got my pile of comics together and put them in a big brown paper bag so the snow wouldn't wet them.

I decided what I would charge Mr. Logg for them if he wanted them and then I headed up Cobourg Street to his place.

I went up the shaky little elevator in the building on the corner of Clarence and Cobourg streets to Mr. Logg's apartment. I got off on the fourth floor and walked down the dark, dirty hallway to his door. The air was hot and lumpy. The radiators were clunking next to the garbage chute. I put my mitts on top of the radiator beside Mr. Logg's door and started knocking. He had a ratty-looking wreath nailed there with a cross-eyed Santa in the middle of it. Mr. Logg was probably asleep and I'd have to knock for quite a while before he'd get up and open the door. He'd be in his underwear and he'd be rubbing his little eyes. I just knew it.

And rubbing his huge unshaven face.

And scratching his big hairy arms.

I kept knocking and watching the steam come off my mitts.

The wreath fell off a couple of times and I had to hang it back up on the rusty nail each time.

I had war comics with covers that I knew he would like. They had pictures of Japs with big yellow buckteeth, about to shove red-hot pokers into girls' faces. The girls had on torn dresses. Or the covers had pictures of ugly German Krauts wearing big shiny black boots with nails in them, about to shove bayonets into girls' throats. The girls had on more ripped and torn dresses.

Mr. Logg opened the door and stood there scratching himself and rubbing his eyes.

"I was asleep," he said.

I checked to see if my mitts were on fire yet and then went into Mr. Logg's apartment. It smelled awful. It smelled like rotten meat or something.

His radiators were clanging so loudly I thought the whole place was going to blow up.

I showed him my *Crime* and *Cop Killer* comics first just to get him warmed up for the Japs and the Krauts.

The first one had a picture on the cover of a guy in an electric chair getting juiced and another guy in a black suit pulling a big switch. Mr. Logg sat down on the edge of his dirty bed and took a long look at the guy getting his reward for killing about a hundred cops. The guy in the electric chair was saying this:

"Aaaaaarrrrgh!"

Mr. Logg studied it for quite a while. Then he looked up at me out of his little eyes.

"I seen this one," he said.

Brilliant man, Mr. Logg. Good idea to get him in with Blue Cheeks for a while to straighten out his grammar.

Mr. Logg scratched his armpits for a while and started studying the second one. It had on the cover a picture of some kind of ghoul with fangs and long fingernails and drool running out of his mouth, laughing and shutting this girl in a torn dress inside an iron maiden, the spikes just starting to stick into her chest and some drops of blood dropping.

Mr. Logg studied this one for quite a while too.

"Seen it," said Mr. Logg, and then he yawned, and his mouth opened wider and wider until he looked like a picture of a hippopotamus I once saw in *National Geographic*.

I was looking around Mr. Logg's room while he was grunting and breathing and trying to figure out which comics he'd read and which he hadn't.

His window was all weepy and stained and dirty. On his dresser he had a photograph of himself when he was young. He was just as ugly then as he was now. On his wall he had a big picture of Jesus with so much blood on it that you could hardly see his face.

He had pictures cut out of the paper, yellow and old-looking, of dead bodies and ambulances and executions.

And he had a big poster on the wall over his bed, a drawing of an evil-looking man in a raggedy cloak with hands like claws and burning eyes and a big hooked nose like a beak.

On the bottom of the poster it had the word JEW! in big black letters.

"Seen it," said Mr. Logg and he put down a *Crime Comic* with a guy shooting a policeman in the face on the cover.

He was getting down the pile. He was into the *Donald Duck* section. He was laughing.

Scrooge McDuck was eating a whole lot of money. Mr. Logg thought that was really funny. He laughed like he was choking.

When he got to the Japs and the red-hot pokers and Krauts and the big black boots he got really excited. He hadn't seen any of them. He started groaning and grunting as he put them in a different pile. He was going to buy those.

There were piles of dirty underwear and socks and rumpled pants sticking out from under his bed. And big fluffy balls of dust along the walls that moved a little bit each time Mr. Logg put a comic book down on one of the piles. The balls of dust rolled a little bit when the air moved. They looked like little tumbleweeds tumbling.

Mr. Logg was staring at a cover showing a soldier's boot crushing a Jap face with big buckteeth and another soldier throwing Japs over a cliff into a big fire.

While Mr. Logg was enjoying himself I felt something tugging at my mind. There was something awful in the room with Mr. Logg and me.

My eyes went back down to the mess under his saggy bed. There was something else there besides dirty clothes and dust balls. I could see the corner of something else there. Not clothes. Cloth. White cloth. White cloth with writing on it. The writing was partly showing. I leaned over a little to read the words. The words were: AND SEED.

My mind was whirling.

My stomach was upside-down.

"What're ya lookin' at?" I heard Mr. Logg's voice say.

I looked up and met his piggy eyes.

"What're ya lookin' at?"

"Nothing," I said in a whisper while his eyes burned me.

"Lookin' at nothin', eh?" Mr. Logg said and went back to his comics.

The pile he was going to buy was growing bigger. I figured there'd be around thirty comics he wanted.

"You think you're pretty smart, don't you?" Mr. Logg said.

I didn't answer. My eyes wanted to leave his but I wouldn't let them.

"How much for these comics here?"

"They're five cents each except the war ones. They're seven cents each," I said, trying not to swallow.

He stood up, and with his heel he kicked the mess under his bed and out of sight. He was smiling his rotten teeth at me as he took a handful of my curly hair in his big hand.

"Seven cents for the war ones, eh? Why seven cents for the war ones?"

He tightened his hold on my hair so that I had to stand on my toes.

"Because they're harder to get," I said.

"Why are they harder to get?" he said.

"Because people like to keep them, I guess," I said, not swallowing.

He tightened his grip. I was way up on my toes. I was hoping I wouldn't have to swallow. It's a sign of being scared when you swallow. Our cat did it all the time. When he was trapped, he'd look up at you and swallow.

I didn't want Mr. Logg to know how scared I was.

I hated him too much.

"Why do people like to keep them?" he said.

"Because they like them."

"But *you* don't like them!"

I didn't answer.

"Why don't you want to keep them?"

"I sell them because I need the money."

His foul breath in my face was going to make me sick.

"Christmas presents."

"Isn't that nice. The smart little business man. Seven

cents for the war ones. Christmas presents. Who's gonna get the nicest present?"

I didn't answer.

"Who?" He jerked my head back.

"A beautiful girl," I said between my teeth.

"A beautiful girl! I thought only sissies had girlfriends! What's her name?"

I couldn't say the name. I couldn't say the name. He could have killed me but I would never have said that name in that room to that man.

"The name, sissy!" He jerked my head again. I was as far up on my toes as I could get.

"The name!"

"Fleurette Featherstone Fitchell!" I said.

"Who?"

"Fleurette Featherstone Fitchell!"

"What a stupid name!" said stupid Mr. Logg and let me go.

He laughed a big horse laugh and went into his bathroom but only closed the door part way.

I waited until I heard his water crashing into the bowl and then I dove under the bed and pulled out the pile of clothes. I spread out the piece with the writing on it. It was a cloth flour bag with eye-holes cut in it. And the writing.

RITCHIE'S FEED AND SEED, it said.

I heard the toilet flush. I shoved the stuff back under the bed and got up just in time and pretended I was looking out his dirty window.

He didn't say anything.

He was acting like I wasn't even there.

We counted the comics. The price came to a dollar seventy. He gave me the exact amount without saying a word. I picked up my leftover comics and quietly left. His face was buried in a war comic when I took a quick glance back. I shut his door quietly. When I shut the door his wreath fell on the floor. I left it there and got my mitts off the radiator.

When I got out on the street I sucked in big gulps of clean winter air.

Back home, under my bed, I had a big supply of paper for writing lines for people at school. I got out a stack of it and counted out two hundred sheets and put them in a neat pile.

I got out my best pencil and in big writing I wrote on the top sheet:

It was Mr. Logg of 32 Cobourg St., Apartment 406, who beat up Sammy Rosenberg's father of 102 Cobourg Street last week in the car barns. I have proof.

Signed

The Shadow

P.S. Merry Christmas.

Then, on the second sheet, I wrote out the same thing. And on the third.

I had finished sheet number fifty when my thumb got so sore I needed a rest. I went downstairs and had a little snack while my thumb was resting. My sister Pamela was at her window watching the snow and Aunt Dottie was finishing up the tree.

Dad was sitting back suggesting where to hang this and where to place that. Aunt Dottie paid no attention and put the decorations wherever she thought they should go. Each icicle was put on separately by Aunt Dottie and smoothed out straight so it would hang properly. Each ball was placed so at least two lights would reflect in it a certain way. Each little bell had to be just above and over to the left of each ball. Each little Santa faced out in one direction at a point on the other wall. Each little daub of fake snow was placed exactly where two branches forked together. Everything went into its own perfect place.

Aunt Dottie was the best tree decorator on the planet Earth.

"When that Frank person arrives here I want you to make sure he doesn't touch this tree," Aunt Dottie was saying.

"Don't worry," Dad said. "Frank never even notices things like that."

"As a matter of fact, I don't want him anywhere near this tree," Aunt Dottie was saying as she polished one of the reflectors with a little tissue.

"We could always lock him in the cellar until it's time for him to go home," Dad said.

"You know very well what I mean," Aunt Dottie said.

They kept talking about Frank while I went back upstairs and wrote the message fifty more times.

I went down again at six o'clock and listened to "Ozzie and Harriet." When "The Great Gildersleeve" came on I left for evensong at St. Albany's. I took fifty blank sheets with me under my coat and a couple of pencils. I could write a few sheets during Reverend Well's sermon.

During the processional the sheets almost slipped out from under my cassock but I caught them between my knees and pretended to almost drop my hymn book. After we sang a couple more hymns Reverend Well got up in his box and got going on his sermon.

There were a few empty seats where some people had stacked their coats. Because this church was very hot people liked to take their coats off. Not like the Dogan church where you had to keep your coat on because it was pretty cool.

Reverend Well's sermon was quite long and I had time to get fifty messages written out.

I looked up to see how the people were doing and I noticed that some of them had flopped onto their coats and were sleeping very heavily. You could hear some snoring and if you looked around you could see that practically everybody was nodding and jerking their heads back up before they hit the pews in front of them.

It must have been the heat.

I got my pay. I ran all the way home through the

snowflakes and got there just in time to catch the last of Charlie McCarthy on the radio.

Then I listened to Fred Allen and went upstairs. But I didn't get undressed. I wrote out fifty more messages.

Waited until the tubes faded in the radio and everybody went to bed.

Then, very quietly, I got dressed warmly and went out to fix Mr. Logg. I had two hundred messages.

I started in Mr. Logg's apartment. I went up the fire escape by the garbage chute and got in the first floor hallway. I slipped one of my messages under each door.

Then I went to the second floor and did the same. And the third. And the fourth. Everybody got one but Mr. Logg. I passed by his door without breathing.

The cross-eyed Santa was hanging there, not following me.

Then I went to all the doors on all the streets around Mr. Logg's place. All of his neighbors got a message. All along Cobourg Street and Papineau and Augusta Street and Friel Street and Clarence Street and York Street until I had only one left.

Not one person saw me.

I was all by myself.

I was invisible.

I was Lamont Cranston. The Shadow.

I had one message left.

I walked down Cobourg Street, over Angel Square, across St. Patrick, and over onto Whitepath Street.

I walked down Whitepath Street to Margot Lane's house and up onto her little verandah.

I put my last message in the mailbox there.

Invisible.

The Shadow.

7 Long Prayer

LAST SHOPPING DAY till Christmas and Woolworth's on Rideau Street was an insane asylum.

I got there at seven in the morning before they opened and worked like a madman bringing stuff up from the basement and putting it on the shelves.

By nine o'clock we had everything stacked neatly in order and in the right place. My job was over at noon. Then I'd get my big pay and I'd be ready to pick up my presents.

They would pay me twelve dollars at noon for four Saturdays.

Our boss asked some of us to come and help him open the doors. There were thousands of people out there, standing in the falling snow. Some of the other workers said that our boss was afraid to open the doors by himself. They said that last year on the last shopping day till Christmas the people knocked our boss down and trampled him.

I noticed, as he put the key in the lock and as all the people's faces pressed up against the glass and breathed fog, that his face was very pale and his eyes were glazed over and he took a huge swallow so that his Adam's apple ran up his throat and back down like a little elevator. He was scared all right.

About an hour later when I saw him he was surrounded by about a hundred shoppers. They were all yelling at him and one of the sleeves was torn off his jacket.

About eleven o'clock, during my break, I got in line with all the little kids to talk to Ozzie O'Driscoll. Santa.

The kids were getting a little wild because it was the last shopping day till Christmas. Some of them were crying and others were pulling on Ozzie's beard. One of the arms of his throne was broken off and there was a big stain on his trousers. I guess one of the kids got too excited while sitting on his knee.

It was the turn of the kid ahead of me.

The one behind me was trying to shove me out of the way.

"You're too big to be here," he kept saying to me as he tried to push me out of line.

I could hear Ozzie O'Driscoll talking to the kid in front of me.

"You were here *twice* before," Ozzie said to the kid.

"No, I wasn't," the kid said. You could tell he was lying because his face was all twisted up like somebody had just made him eat a lemon.

"Yes, you were," Ozzie said. "I even remember what you wanted. A tank."

"A *real* tank," the kid said.

"I can't *get* a real tank in my *sleigh*, I told you. Real tanks are bigger than my sleigh. I told you that before."

"Get a bigger sleigh!" the kid said.

"I can't get a bigger sleigh. I've got only a few hours left before I take off. And I've got to get all the way up to the North Pole. I just haven't got the time."

"Tell Mrs. Claus to do it."

"Mrs. Claus is too busy. And anyway, even if she wasn't busy, she wouldn't do it."

"Why not?"

"Because she hates me. I'm never home."

"My dad says you're a fake," the kid said, with his chin stuck out.

"Well, ask your dad for the tank then!"

I knelt down beside Ozzie O'Driscoll's throne and put my mouth to his ear. His beard tickled me while I told him all about Mr. Logg. I told him about Sammy's father and about how I saw the hood under Mr. Logg's bed and how I put all the messages in everybody's place and how Mr. Logg pulled my hair and how he tried to make me say Margot Lane's name and how I wouldn't.

I told him everything.

Ozzie looked at me. His eyes got very serious. He told me I had done a very brave thing and he told me not to worry. He said he was going into the police station that night and he would get the Sergeant to send somebody over to Mr. Logg's to investigate. He said they might not be able to arrest him but they could put him under investigation and throw a good scare into him so that he wouldn't dare try to hurt anybody again.

Anyway, he would try.

At noon I got my pay and ran over to Freiman's.

I found the Virgin Mary lady and paid for the rest of Margot's Richard Hudnut Three Flower Gift Set.

I went up to Sparks Street to Laura Secord's and got Aunt Dottie her chocolates. The box said, "Old Time Home Made Laura Secord Candies."

Beside the writing on the white box was a picture of the crabbiest-looking lady I've ever seen. It was Laura Secord. Her mouth was turned down on each end and her eyes were narrow slits and her nose had a hook on it just like a parrot's. She had on a white hat pulled down over her head and tied so tight under her chin that she looked like she was choking. On the side of the box was a picture of her gravestone at Queenston Heights. The gravestone looked happier than she did.

But her chocolates were the best in the world, so she must have been a nice person.

I went to the Joke Shop on Bank Street and bought

Gerald a big rubber cigar for when we played gangster movies.

I went down to Ogilvy's on Rideau Street and bought Sammy a repeater cap gun and two boxes of caps.

Then I went to Prevost on Cobourg Street and bought Coco Laframboise a private detective's badge. For his detecting.

I went in the house and my sister Pamela gave me a big hug and I put my finger to my lips and tried to make her understand that I had presents and that there were secrets and I sneaked up the stairs on my toes with my finger on my lips and she stood at the bottom of the stairs with her head on one side and her eyes shining and her face like a big question mark.

It was like when a puppy looks at you. Trying to understand. Almost understanding the mystery.

Dad was mixing up a big bowl of punch and another big jug of eggnog and Aunt Dottie was preparing the Mock Duck, tying it up with lots of strong string.

I wrapped my presents and put my sister Pamela's yellow duck and Aunt Dottie's chocolates and Dad's Flat Fifty under the tree and then I went out into the Lowertown Christmas Eve to CoCo's house.

Mrs. Laframboise let me in and I could smell pies baking and CoCo gave me a present and I gave him his. I opened mine. It was a picture of The Shadow in his cloak and his big black hat. It was autographed.

We had some Nesbitt Orange to celebrate and I

wished everybody a Merry Christmas and CoCo put on his badge and I went out into the beautiful snow and all the warm windows glowing yellow along Cobourg Street and went over to Gerald Hickey's house and gave him his present and he gave me mine. It was a beautiful book of Shadow stories with a picture of The Shadow on the front in his black cloak and his big black hat with the brim down over his face and Margot Lane looking at him with her big eyes. And Gerald and I had some Honey Dew to celebrate and he put his rubber cigar in the corner of his mouth and shot me all the way out onto the street.

And we shouted Merry Christmas to each other and I went up to Sammy's apartment and knocked on the door.

I knocked again.

The hall was dark and there was some singing coming from another apartment down the hall and some laughing.

But nobody answered Sammy's door.

That night I went to bed early.

And I tried a prayer.

I had never tried a prayer before.

I prayed for a nice time.

A time when nobody thought some other person's face was funny to look at and nobody laughed at other people's parents and said they were stupid-looking and nobody made fun of the way they talked and nobody thought somebody else wore funny-looking clothes or hateful clothes.

And nobody got beat up because of the kind of hat they wore or because they were poor or because of the street they lived on.

And nobody got spit on because they had different kinds of food in their lunch or their father came to meet them after school with a long coat on and maybe a beard.

And nobody got their mitts stolen or got tripped in the snow because their names didn't sound right or they believed in some other kind of religion or read a different kind of bible or had freckles on their faces or had the wrong kind of hair or had to go home at a different time from school or didn't have skates or *did* have skates or weren't allowed to play alleys on Saturday or on Sunday or *were*, or got dunked in water at church or didn't swear or *did* swear or smelled funny or couldn't eat fish or *had* to eat fish or wore a hat in church or *didn't* wear a hat in church or said the Lord's Prayer different or *didn't* say the Lord's Prayer at all.

And nobody got punched in the mouth because they had clean fingernails or fat lips or couldn't understand English or couldn't speak French or couldn't pronounce Hebrew.

And there were no gangs waiting all the time, so nobody had to go down different streets just to get to the store or go to school.

And you could carry a book along with you or a

mouth organ or something and people wouldn't take it from you and then tear it into pieces or grab it and smash it up against a wall.

A time when you maybe liked a girl and they wouldn't come along and twist your arm behind your back and try and make you say dirty things about her.

A nice time.

That's what I prayed for.

The prayer might work, I thought.

Or it might not.

It was a mystery.

8 Happy, Happy

CHRISTMAS MORNING we had the Quaker with brown sugar and cream instead of milk. My sister Pamela had trouble eating the brown sugar because she still didn't know what it was. She still wasn't used to it even though the war was over.

Then we went and sat around Aunt Dottie's perfect tree and opened up our presents. I opened up a new hat with fur on the forehead and fur ear flaps. My sister Pamela opened up her little yellow duck. We showed her how to squeeze it again, just like last year, to make it quack. It went quack for her just like last year. And she laughed and was happy all over again. Then I opened a present with new socks in it and a new sweater. Then Dad picked up his present from me and weighed it in his hands and felt the shape of it.

"I hope it's a Flat Fifty!" he said and ripped the paper off.

"It is! It is a Flat Fifty! Just what I wanted! Thank you very much!"

And while Aunt Dottie was taking such a long time to open hers (she wouldn't tear the paper) Dad said, "I wonder if it's chocolates!" And when she finally got it open, he shouted, "It is! It's chocolates! Let's have a couple!"

"You're not having any. I'm saving these for myself for a change this year," Aunt Dottie said. And she put them down beside her.

And then we all had a couple.

I got new boots and new breeks and new mitts and a new scarf. And Aunt Dottie got a book about poetry from Dad.

After Dad opened up some handkerchiefs and a tie and some socks and Aunt Dottie opened up some new rubber gloves and a new apron and some ribbon, there was only Sammy's present sitting under the tree all by itself.

Downstairs in the cellar while I was getting some shortbread with the half-cherry on each piece wrapped in the waxpaper, I could hear the sad sound of my sister's yellow duck quacking.

While we were having a little snack Dad turned on the radio and we listened to King George's Christmas message from England. It was quite static and his voice sounded very thin and lonely. He was so far away. Dad said that he sounded like that because he was very sick and he was going to die soon, he thought.

Not happy.

That afternoon I was sitting with my sister Pamela looking out her window. I was waiting for a feeling to come over me so I could take Margot's present over to her. I couldn't take it over there with the feeling I had on me. I wanted to feel like I did on the night of the moon eclipse. A good feeling.

Suddenly Sammy appeared out of the snow and knocked on our door. My sister Pamela and I got to the door at the same time and we nearly killed him with our hugs.

He told me that his father woke up in the hospital in Toronto and that he was going to be all right. His big brown eyes were full of water.

I gave Sammy his Christmas present even though it wasn't Christmas for him and he gave me mine. We both opened them at the same time. They were exactly the same thing.

Two repeater cap guns with two extra boxes of caps.

I told him all about Mr. Logg and the messages I sent and Ozzie O'Driscoll. I told him everything.

He said there were some people hanging around outside Mr. Logg's and that he saw a police car there when he came by to my place.

We ran up Cobourg Street and joined the crowd.

Gerald was there and so was CoCo. And a big crowd of people. There was a police car parked along the snowbank and the people were looking at the car and looking up at Mr. Logg's window on the fourth floor. The snow was floating down.

"They say Mr. Logg didn't go to war because he's a coward," said a lady in a black hat.

"They say Mr. Logg kills little kids and he eats dem," said CoCo Laframboise.

"They say he reads comics all the time and his I.Q. is zero," said a man who was interested in measuring intelligence.

"They say The Shadow is going to get a medal," said Gerald. "Or at least a nice reward."

"Who *is* The Shadow, anyway?" said another lady.

"They say it's Tommy, down the street."

"You mean *this* Tommy?" said a man, pointing at me.

"It's not me," I said.

"They say people are putting in money to help Sammy's father pay the hospital," somebody else said.

"He's a Jew," somebody else said. "Nobody would do that for a Jew!"

"They say Mr. Logg has horns and a tail."

"They say he's afraid to come out."

Just then the apartment building door opened and the policeman came out.

"Aren't you going to arrest Mr. Logg?"

"No, I just came to ask him a few questions," the

policeman said as he climbed over the snowbank and opened the door of his car.

"He's guilty as sin!" a lady shouted.

"No he's not," said somebody else.

"They say The Shadow found the evidence!"

The policeman shut his door and started his motor.

"Mr. Logg should be very careful," said a great big man about the size of Uncle Paddy. "Somebody might do the same thing to him someday!"

"Jews should be beat up," somebody said.

The police car pulled quietly away in the soft falling snow.

"Mr. Logg is a hog," said a small, quiet man.

Then everybody looked up at Mr. Logg's window.

It was opening.

And out came his ugly head.

"Come down you slimy coward!" said the man as big as Uncle Paddy.

"You're the one! You're the one who hit Sammy's father over the head, you filthy monster!" shouted the lady in the black hat.

"Get away from here! Get away from here! You have no proof!" said Mr. Logg's ugly mouth.

"We don't need proof, we know what you're like!" shouted another lady.

"He's innocent," said somebody else.

"It's true," said the quiet man, "there is no *real* proof. It's not right to accuse a person unless you have proof."

"The Shadow has proof," I said.

"How do *you* know?"

"Because he told me."

"He told you. You know this Shadow?"

"Yes."

"Who is he?"

"I can't tell. But he saw the Ritchie's Feed and Seed bag under Mr. Logg's bed."

"It's under your bed, the evidence is!" shouted the big man up at Mr. Logg.

Suddenly the window slammed shut. For a minute nobody said or did anything.

Then my best Pea Soup friend, CoCo Laframboise, detective, solved it.

"Round da back. He'll trow it in de garbage. It will come down de chute at de back!"

Everybody ran down the laneway of the apartment building to the back and crowded into the garbage room to watch the bottom of the chute.

Sure enough, we heard something slam away up above, and something came bumping and hissing down the metal chute.

Out came a brown paper bag. CoCo grabbed it almost before it hit the bin and tore it open. Egg shells, tea leaves, bean cans, garbage. Nothing but garbage.

But wait! Underneath it all, rolled up in a tight ball, was the Ritchie's Feed and Seed hood. Everybody let out a big cheer.

Right after I got home Dad's friend Frank arrived. I was coming downstairs after making sure Margot's present was all right.

Frank was in the hall trying to take his army boots off so he wouldn't dirty Aunt Dottie's floors.

He was standing on one foot trying to undo the lace of his boot. Then he started hopping. Then he lost his balance totally. He leaned on the door that went into the front room and the door opened and Frank went running and falling sideways in there. There was a tall floor lamp there and Frank grabbed it by the skinny neck but it wouldn't hold him so he let it go and it crashed on the floor. Frank was falling near the window now and had his hands full of our curtains. When the curtains gave way he went for some pictures on the wall and a bowl of nuts on the fake mantelpiece. Things were crashing all over the place and Aunt Dottie, who was in the kitchen reading her book on poetry, came out to see Frank aiming himself backwards towards our big armchair.

Frank missed the chair and came quite fast into the little living room pulling down all the Christmas streamers and tipping our dish cabinet as he headed for the tree.

"Not the tree!" Aunt Dottie said and went back into the kitchen just as Frank stomped on the unwrapped presents. Then he turned around, out of control, and dove headfirst into the Christmas tree.

Only Frank's legs stuck out from the mess in the cor-

"His I.Q. must be *less* than zero," said the I.Q. man.

Around the front again, the big man as big as Uncle Paddy sent me up the hydro post about six rungs to tie the proof right where Mr. Logg would see it from his window.

"Hooray for The Shadow, whoever he is!" shouted the quiet man while I was still up the post. And everybody looked up at me and shouted, "Hooray for The Shadow, whoever he is!"

In the crowd I could see Fleurette Featherstone Fitchell. She was looking up at me.

"Thanks, Fitchy!" I shouted.

"Hooray for The Shadow!" shouted Fleurette Featherstone Fitchell. And she had a nice look on her face as she looked at me.

And I thought I saw Mr. Logg at his window but I wasn't sure. And I didn't care if he saw me there or not, because he couldn't hurt me now, there were too many neighbors who knew he was guilty.

Neighbors in Lowertown, Ottawa.

I said goodbye to CoCo and Gerald and Sammy. I said I had something important to do and I'd see them later. They said *they* had an important message to deliver and that they'd see *me* later. I wondered for a minute what they meant but I didn't think of it anymore and went right home for the Mock Duck.

Now I had the feeling.

ner and some smoke came up from the lights because of short circuits.

After we got everything cleaned up and Dad got the lights to work on the tree again and got Frank straightened out and I helped Aunt Dottie set the table we sat down to eat our Christmas dinner (sipper).

I asked if it would be all right if I ate quickly and left because I had a present to deliver.

"Who's it for?" Aunt Dottie asked.

"A girl," I said.

"Isn't that nice," Aunt Dottie said. She was glaring at Frank.

"Isn't that nice," Dad said.

"Yes," Frank said, pulling a piece of string as long as his arm from his throat that he'd eaten with the Mock Duck. "Isn't that nice!"

I walked slowly across Angel Square and up Whitepath Street towards Margot Lane's house. The snow was falling like it does in one of those round glass balls that you shake. There was nobody on the street because it was supper time. The streetlight made the flakes around it look like little silver flies.

If I looked back I could see my tracks. There were no tracks up Margot's walk and no tracks on her steps. The verandah light was on and there was a wreath on the door.

I was the only boy in the world.

I stood on her verandah and rang the bell. I had the present in my hand.

She opened the door and the warm light knifed out across me. Some bells on the wreath on the door shook out a little tune. I could see the reflection of part of their Christmas tree in a mirror in the hall behind her.

I held out the present.

"This is a present for you for Christmas, Margot Lane," I said.

She took the present and slowly closed the door until it was only open a crack wide enough for her lips.

"Thank you, Shadow," she whispered.

"I'm not The Shadow," I said.

"Yes, you are. You are Lamont Cranston, The Shadow. And you did a very brave thing."

"How did you find out?"

"Your friends CoCo and Gerald and Sammy told me. That's how I know. Everybody knows."

"Would you come for a walk with me tomorrow?" I said, my voice sounding like Lamont's.

"Yes I would, Shadow," she whispered.

Then she softly closed the door.

I went down from her verandah and ran all the way home. Across Angel Square.

The snow had stopped. And the moon, peeking out, followed me as I ran.

Happy.

Happy!

Happy Christmas.

People in the Book

Sammy's father – An innocent man who was hurt because of hatred.

Dad – Dad.

Aunt Dottie – A very clean and nice woman.

Mr. Aubrey – A butcher who was lucky to still have his thumb.

Sammy – My best Jew friend.

Mr. Blue Cheeks – The worst teacher on the planet Earth.

The lovely Margot Lane – The Shadow's companion on the radio.

The Shadow – Alias Lamont Cranston, wealthy young man-about-town, fighter of crime and rooter-out of evil.

The Quaker – A man on a box of porridge who saw everywhere at once.

Toe-Jam Laframboise – The delivery man whose socks were on forever.

My sister Pamela – An angel who couldn't know anything.

The cat – Our cat.
Margot Lane herself – The only girl in the world.
Miss Strong – A teacher who laughed at people who wanted to be writers.
Miss Frack and Miss Eck – Two robins.
Albert Einstein – An inventor.
Melody Bleach – The worst writer in the class.
Ralph – A moose stole his camera.
Geranium Mayburger – Dumb.
CoCo Laframboise – My best Pea Soup friend.
Killer Bodnoff – The toughest Jew.
Manfred Mahoney – The toughest Dogan.
Denny Trail – A Protestant who moved.
Arnold Levinson – The sissiest Jew.
Telesphore Bourgignon – The sissiest Pea Soup.
Clary O'Mara – The sissiest Dogan.
Sherwood Ashbury – The sissiest Protestant.
Anita Pleet – The smartest girl.
Martha Banting – The nicest girl.
Fleurette Featherstone Fitchell – The hamburger bun artist.
Delbert Dilabio – A horseball head.
Mr. Maynard – The best teacher in the universe.
Steve Wilson and Loreli Kilbourne – They were on the radio in "Big Town".
Sir John A. Macdonald – The Father of Confederation.
Gerald Hickey – My best Dogan friend.
Father Francis – A teacher with long arms.

Arnie Sultzburger – Dad was going to kill him.
Lester Lister – A friend of mine I didn't like.
Uncle Paddy – My favorite uncle with the big feet.
Mr. and Mrs. Lister and Esther – People that rhyme.
Turkeys – Secret weapons.
Chalmers Lonnigan – A person who wanted to go to heaven early.
Morrison-Lamothe – Our breadman who smelled like bread.
Ozzie O'Driscoll – Santa Claus on his holidays.
Mrs. Claus – A fed-up wife.
Uncle Jim and Captain Marvel – Two of Santa's reindeer.
Mock Duck – A pretend turkey.
Laurel and Hardy – They eat socks.
Frank – Back from the war with poor balance.
Red Cap – Dad's cousin from up the Ga-Ga-Gatineau.
Bing Crosby – A singer who makes Christmas feel right.
Rita Hayworth – A model.
Richard Hudnut – A present manufacturer.
Virgin Mary – A saleslady.
Doll – An Imbro's waitress.
Louis – The owner of the place.
Tony Janero and Humberto Zavala – They stopped fighting because of the tubes.
Snowman – A practice torture victim.
Abbot and Costello – People who eat furniture.
U-Wanta Waitress – She thought Gerald was dead.
Buffalo – His eyes are made of glass.

Commissionaire — A quiet guard (sometimes).
The Art Expert — His hair was his main interest.
High-pants — The hero, blown up till next week.
The girl — Useless but nice.
Mr. Logg — A bad man.
Mr. and Mrs. McIntosh — They disagreed about electrocution.
Father Foley — A very elegant dresser.
Jesus —
Reverend Well — A long speaker.
Laura Secord — A nice lady, mean face.
Mrs. Laframboise — A detective's mother.
King George — A far-way and lonesome king.
A Crowd of Neighbors — Good for Angel Square.

Franklin Pierce College Library
00160427